Catching Chase

A Second-Chance Romance Novel

by

Michelle Windsor

Copyright © Michelle Windsor 2020
Michelle Windsor asserts the right to be identified as the author of this work.

*****

All rights reserved. No part of this book may be reproduced, scanned, distributed, or sold in any printed or electronic form without direct, written permission from the author. Please do not participate in piracy of copyrighted materials in violation of the author's rights.

*****

This is a work of fiction. All names, characters, places, and incidents are products of the author's imagination and are used fictionally, and any resemblance to actual persons, living or dead, businesses, companies, events, or locales is entirely coincidental.

For my husband, Doug.
For teaching me to love the game.
And for your endless love and support.

Prologue

I give a final wave as I step away from the podium at the front of the room, then make my way over to the steps leading off of the stage. I've just completed the last presentation required of me at my company's annual conference, and could not be more relieved. It's been a grueling four days of interaction as I tried to impress present and hopefully new clients with our products, and now I'm looking forward to some much needed downtime.

I weave my way out of the room as quickly as I can, only being stopped twice along the way to answer questions, heaving a sigh of relief when I reach the exit doors and push through them. I head in the direction of the elevators, my heels echoing across the tiled lobby floor when I hear my name being called.

"Megan?" I'm not sure if I'm the Megan in question, so I plant the toe of my shoe and spin in the direction of the voice. I freeze in place when my eyes connect with the person calling out my name.

"Megan! It is you." My heart rate accelerates, my pulse thundering in my ears so loud I can barely hear what he says next. "I almost didn't recognize you with your short hair." He's reached me now, and I still haven't uttered a word. I just stare at him in complete shock, a frown tarnishing his perfect lips as he points to himself. "It's Jasper. Please tell me you remember me."

I finally gather my senses and offer him a smile. "Of course I remember you." I lean forward, my fingers gripping his bicep in a loose hold as I brush an awkward kiss against his smooth cheek. I've never been this close to him when he's clean shaven. "I was just surprised to see you."

His hand sweeps against the blunt ends of my locks, just grazing the top of my shoulders. "Besides the hair, you haven't changed a bit." My hand releases his arm as I step back, my eyes fixating on his as my brain tries to catch up with my pulse. "What are you doing in Boston?"

"I'm here for a conference." I swing my gaze around the room, trying to find an exit strategy. "What about you?"

"I'm in town for the marathon. I'm meeting a couple of the guys for lunch." He shakes his head, sweeping a hand over the broad smile that's lighting up his face, like he's trying to either hide or contain his joy. "I can't believe it's really you. What's it been? Three years?"

"Almost four." I respond immediately, knowing exactly how long it's been. "Look, Jasper, I have to run, but it was lovely seeing you."

His brow creases at my obvious attempt to cut things

short, not giving me the satisfaction as he tries to extend our reunion. "How long are you in town for? Do you want to have dinner tonight and catch up?" He glances for a moment at his feet, which are shifting back and forth in place, then continues. "I've wondered about you a lot over the years." He meets me in the eye, his tone becoming quiet. "There are things I'd like to say and explain."

My heart catches in my throat as I swallow down the feelings lodged there. I force a small smile to play on my lips. "Unfortunately, I'm heading up to my room now to gather my things to check out."

"Can I convince you to stay?" His palm is against my cheek before I can react, the memory of his skin against my own sending a jolt of pain to my very core.

I take a step back, his hand falling to his side as I shake my head. "I'm so sorry." I retreat another step. "I already have an obligation that can't be changed."

"Oh." His brow creases again as his lips curve downward. "Well, are you still in New York? I really would love to see you now that I've found you again."

"I really don't think that's a good idea." I walk away from him, trying to be as polite as I can without breaking into a run in an attempt to escape. "I'm sorry, but I really do have to go."

Unfortunately, he's not giving up that easily, and follows after me. "Megan, wait."

I pause mid-stride, closing my eyes in the hope that I can erase what's happening right now, opening them when I feel his hand wrap around mine to stop me. "Did I do something wrong?"

I turn to meet his eyes; his beautiful, unique eyes, and respond in a whisper. "No."

"Are you married?" He glances down to my hands, bare of any rings, then back to my gaze.

I can't help the short guff of laughter that tumbles from me at the irony of his question, releasing his hand. "No."

"Then what is it?" He pleads, wanting answers that I don't want to give. That I can't give. Not now. He's three years too late.

"Momma!" A voice I know better than any other calls excitedly from behind me, spiking the anxiety I was already feeling into near panic. Goosebumps prickle over every inch of my skin as I realize what's about to happen. Little arms wrap around my legs seconds later in a hug, his sweet voice muffled against my thigh as he says Momma again. I'm frozen like a deer caught in headlights, unable to look away from Jasper as his face displays several emotions in a row; surprise, shock, confusion, and then anger as they meet mine again. I lift my son to rest him on my hip, his eyes a mirror image of the man staring at us both, realization dawning across his features as his fingers splay over his gaping mouth.

In that same moment, my mother appears beside me, a little out of breath, but not so much that she can't chastise the boy in my arms. "Bennet Montgomery Lewis! How many times do I have to tell you not to run away from Grandma like that?"

Jasper's wide eyes ricochet to mine. "His name is Bennet?"

"What's going on?" My mother's head snaps back and

forth as she tries to understand what's transpiring, a gasp bursting from her when she sees the resemblance between Jasper and Bennet.

I nod, blinking rapidly to try and stop the tears that are threatening to spill from my water-rimmed eyes. *How is this happening right now? And why? Why now after all this time?*

Chapter One
─────────

Three and a half years earlier…

I step out of the Uber onto the sidewalk in front of the hotel I'm staying at, pausing to tilt my face up to the sun. It's only seventy degrees, but much more pleasant than I'm used to in January. I smile through the heat warming my cheeks, knowing from a conversation I had earlier with my office, that it's snowing in New York. You can bet I didn't register one complaint when they asked me to come to Los Angeles for the week.

I hum out a contented sigh, open my eyes, then turn to push through the revolving door into the lobby, my heels screeching to a halt as I absorb the sight before me. Men. In suits. Lots of them. All large in stature. Before I even have time to blink to make sure I'm not dreaming, a hard body slams into me from behind, a yelp of surprise bursting from me as I fly forward. Every one of those well-dressed men turn their heads in my direction when the folders I'm holding spill out of my arms and scatter across the marble floor in front of them.

"For Christ's sake Chase, don't you look where you're going?" One of the men in the lobby shakes his head, stretching his arms out to point in my direction. "Look what you did to this poor woman."

It's then, when the heat from his response blows against my neck, that I register the strong fingers gripped around my waist, tightening as they shift me into a stable position. "I obviously didn't expect anyone to be standing smack in the middle of the doorway asshole." His hold releasing as he moves beside me, his gaze locking onto mine, his voice lowering. "Pardon my language." This clearly directed at me and not the other man, as his attention stays focused on me. "Are you alright? I'm sorry about that. I didn't see you."

Jesus, Joseph, and Mary. This man is gorgeous. And has manners to boot. I blink twice, making sure I haven't walked into some kind of dream. I nod and hum out something resembling "uh-huh", too tongue tied by surprise and his beauty to speak any real words. My cheeks heat and in an effort to hide my embarrassment, I bend to begin retrieving my scattered files. He follows suit, sweeping papers into a neat pile, his fingers brushing against mine, startling me again, my eyes darting up to his. I feel my head tilt as the most unique colored irises I've ever seen lock onto mine, leaving me mesmerized. They remind me of the caramel squares I used to eat as a child. The ones often found at the grocery store, individually wrapped in clear cellophane, that you could buy in bulk. The thick, dark lashes framing them are in such contrast to the light color, it's difficult to say with certainty if they are hazel, brown or gold. The dark flecks of green and brown scattered around his pupils actually provide a shimmering effect when he blinks, dazing me further.

One side of his mouth quirks up in a smile, dimples somehow appearing, even though there's a thick beard lining his face, my heartbeat stuttering in response as he speaks, his voice lower this time. "I really am sorry."

I finally snap to my senses and say something to the poor man. "It's my fault. I shouldn't have been standing in the doorway. So, I fear I'm the one that actually owes you an apology."

I move to push myself off the floor at the exact same time he leans forward to help me up, our foreheads meeting in the middle with a hard thunk, stars appearing in my vision from the impact. I slap a hand over the spot where we collided and let out my second yelp of the day as I straighten, glaring at him as I do. Laughter rings loud from the hoard of men watching our every move from the lobby, a few comments thrown out referring to smooth moves and what a jackass my would-be-gentleman is.

"What in the hell is wrong with you?" I hiss. I've had enough and finally lose my patience. "Are you always this much of a klutz?"

His brows shoot north, his entire body jerking back in shock. "I'm the klutz?"

"First you run into me, and then you smack your head into mine, so yes, I'd say you're lacking the basic motor skills that usually keeps one in their own lane."

One of the men in the crowd lets out a low whistle then

laughs. "Guess she must have seen you play in last week's game, eh, Chase?"

He points in the direction of his friend. "Shut it White." His glare shifts to me, the files he's still holding thrust toward me. "Here."

I snatch the pile from his outstretched fingers, add them to the stack I'm holding, then stride purposely away in the direction of the elevators.

"You're welcome." His voice booming over the noise my heels are making against the marble floor, sarcasm lacing every syllable.

I halt, then whirl around, my eyes squinting at him in disbelief. "You're welcome?" I take several steps needed to close the gap between us, the blood boiling in my veins as I approach. "Are you kidding me right now?" His mouth opens to speak, but before he can get a word out, I seethe between clenched teeth. "You slam into me, spill my files everywhere, then smack your head into mine, all while your little frat brothers watch on the sidelines, and you expect me to say thank you?"

His mouth quirks up in a lazy smile, his head shaking once back and forth before he speaks, quietly, so only I can hear him. "Well aren't you just a little spitfire?"

"What did you call me?" I splutter, taken aback by his response, so completely opposite of what I was expecting.

His reply comes only after his lips form a wide smile, his caramel gaze practically sparkling with mischief. "You've got one fiery little temper on you." I stare at him, not sure if it's because his eyes have put me into some kind of trance, or because I'm just not sure how to respond. Either way, it doesn't matter, because he keeps speaking. "My mom always said never argue with a girl with spitfire spirit. Now I understand why."

I squint suspiciously at him, trying to figure out what his angle is. One minute I want to strangle him, and the next, I find myself looking at his lips wondering what they would feel like against mine. And what kind of guy quotes his mother for God's sake? "Yeah, well, your mother was right."

"I know." He smile grows broader. "Which is why I'm not saying another thing."

"You're weird." I state, matter-of-factly, my eyes traveling the length of his well-dressed frame before looking him in the eyes again. "Even if you are cute." Before things get even stranger, I give him one final shake of my head, turning my back to him as I walk into the elevator. As the doors start to close, I spin around, a reluctant smile breaking free when I realize he's still rooted in place, still watching me. When the doors clunk together, I roll my eyes and laugh out loud. "Weirdo."

"Hi Jim." I greet the bartender as I plop into one of the stools surrounding the near empty hotel bar. It's not the first time I've stayed at this hotel on business, and not the first time I've visited his bar. It is the first time however, that I've been down this week, so when his eyes light up in recognition as he smiles back at me, I admit it's nice to be remembered.

"Hello to you too, Megan." He moves to stand in front of me, handing me a wine menu. "It's been a little while."

"Yep." I nod, opening the little black folder to browse the white wine section. "About six weeks or so." I look up and give him a warm smile. "And I think, if I'm lucky, this may be my last trip here for a while. I'm doing the client's product implementation and training this week."

"Ah, lucky for you perhaps, but not me." He shoots me a quick smile. "You're one of the prettiest guests to brighten my bar."

I glance down at the worn jeans and white t-shirt I changed into after going to my room, then back up at Jim. "Not sure how that could possibly be true, but thanks." I give him a gracious smile, my fingers playing with the long, braided plait sitting over my shoulder. I should probably cut it. The blonde, wavy locks have grown almost to my waist, and as much as I love it, it's also always in my way. If it's not piled on top of my head in a messy bun, or in some kind of ponytail, it gets caught in zippers, or stuck under my body when I sleep, or worse, spills into whatever food I'm eating when I lean forward.

"Believe it." Jim states, bringing me back to the here and now, instead of the 'hair now' thoughts I'm pondering. "Just a drink with me tonight, or do I get you for dinner too?" He flirts playfully as he slides a maroon cocktail napkin across the dark wood of the bar in front of me.

"You get the whole package tonight, Jim." I smile coyly, playing along with him. "I've had dinner alone in my room the last two nights and could use some good company."

"Could I try and include myself in that mix?" Jim's attention transfers to the deep voice over my shoulder, one brow quirking up as the interloper continues. "At the very least, maybe buy you a drink to apologize for earlier?"

His movements are slow as he gauges my reaction, the muscled cords of his arms flexing as he eases himself into the stool beside me. I think he's prepared to spring up and away if I utter the slightest negative response. I feel my head nodding in approval though, my lips betraying any kind of rejection I may have tried to feign. I take a second to appreciate his looks again, no less appealing now that he's out of the suit he was in earlier, and in a simple pair of dark jeans and t-shirt. And even though I hate to admit it, he looks even more delicious dressed like this. It doesn't hurt that the tight cotton he's wearing molds perfectly to his chest, the bumps lining his abdomen prominent when he leans back in the stool.

I nod my permission, then swivel my stool to face Jim. "I'll take a champagne please."

"Your usual bottle of Veuve?" His eyes gleam devilishly as he responds. Because this is a running joke between the two of us. I only ever order a glass, even though it's my favorite, always commenting that a bottle is too expensive, but smart enough to know that if this guy is apologizing for something, he's going to make him pay.

I smirk, and toss him a wink. "That would be perfect."

Chapter Two

Yep, she's a spitfire. No doubt about it. And that little interaction she just shared with the bartender proves it. There is no way she regularly drinks a bottle of anything. She's got to be a hundred-twenty pounds soaking wet. But I don't mind playing this game with her. Not only is she beautiful, I love that she's not intimidated by me in the least. And most women are, especially once they find out what I do for a living, and how much money I make.

The bartender strolls over to a walk-in cooler to retrieve the champagne, so I figure I better take advantage of us being alone while the moment exists. "I really would like to apologize for this afternoon."

Her eyes, a deep blue color that reminds me of a twilight sky reflecting against the ocean just after the sun sets, drift up to mine. "For which part?" She teases, a smile tugging at the corners of her lips. "Crashing into me." She lifts her hand and displays two fingers like she's making the peace sign, "twice. Or for your little frat brothers' comments, or for calling me a spitfire?" She rolls her eyes as she gives me a little head shake, the smile on her face making it obvious she's teasing me.

There's a small pop further down the bar as the bottle of champagne is opened, and I chuckle, recognizing the dramatic effect it just gave to her line of questions. Her brows arch high at my reaction. "You think it's funny?"

And of course, that makes me want to laugh more, but I tamp it down and smile broadly instead. "I think that as beautiful as you look angry, it's the last thing I want to make you, so definitely not laughing at you."

"Uh-huh." She drawls, clearly not convinced.

"I have an idea." I decide a new approach is required and stand up to leave. "I think we need to start over." Without another word, I turn and walk out of the bar.

I stand outside the entrance, making sure I'm out of sight, count to sixty, then stride as casually as I possibly can up to the bar where she's sitting. Her eyes are glued to me, watching every move I make, curiosity furrowing her brow. I point to the stool next to her. "Pardon me, is this seat taken?"

She laughs. And it's perfect. Soft and feminine and sexy. Her laughter converts to a smile so breathtaking, I know I want to make her do it again and again. She gives a quick shake of her head. "Nope. It's all yours."

I slide into the seat, still warm from my earlier occupation of it, and turn to meet her eyes. "Can I buy you a drink?"

"Sure." She rolls her eyes dramatically, but through a

large smile, so I know this is okay. "How about a glass a champagne?"

"How about a bottle?" I suggest, looking at the bartender, who's standing across the bar from us again, the open bottle of Veuve in one hand, a curious look on his face as he plays catchup.

"What the hell." She lets out another laugh, tossing a hand in the air. "Jim, I'll take that bottle of Veuve please."

"Okay." His response coming out slow as he tries to figure out what the hell happened while he stepped away. He fills a flute with champagne and then places it in front of her, before reaching for another flute for me.

I wave off the drink. "I'll just have an ice water please."

Her head tilts in my direction. "You won't have a glass with me?"

"I'm training." I leave it at that for now, changing the subject by extending my hand to her. "I'm Jasper, by the way."

She lifts her hand then slowly slips it into mine, squinting as she stares back at me. "Earlier, your friends called you Chase?"

"I thought we were supposed to be meeting for the first time?" I chuckle, but clarify. "Jasper Chase. Those morons are my teammates."

"Ah, okay."

She starts to slide her hand out of mine, but I tighten my grasp, holding it prisoner, her fingers tensing in response until my next question explains why. "And you are?"

Her hand relaxes inside mine, her head tilting slightly, a smile lifting her cheeks. "Megan Lewis."

I release her hand and lift my glass of water to click it against the rim of her flute, making sure my eyes find hers. "It's really nice to meet you Megan Lewis."

"Nice to meet you too, Jasper Chase." She raises her glass, stopping midway to its destination, tilting it toward me. "Cheers."

"Cheers." I smile around my glass as I take another sip of my water, watching as she takes a taste from the flute, her eyes closing for a brief moment as she hums out her approval. "Good?"

"Very." She takes another drink, longer this time, then sets the glass on the napkin in front of her. "Thank you."

"My pleasure." And I mean it. I could watch her wrap those luscious lips around anything, anytime. I shift in my seat, trying to hide the physical reaction starting to happen below my waist at the very thought. Sweet Jesus this woman is sexy, and she isn't even aware of it. Which of course makes her even more so. I definitely appreciated her legs and perfectly round ass in the fitted dress she was in earlier, but even in jeans she's stunning.

"So, teammates?" Her voice interrupting my thoughts. "I should assume it's for some kind of sport and not chess?"

"What, we don't look like we know how to work a board?" I joke, knowing full well that even well-dressed, we are quite the burly bunch.

Her eyes roam over my form before she replies, one brow arching high. "I think you're missing a pocket protector and geeky eyewear."

It's a good thing she can't see what's happening between my pockets, otherwise she just might be running for some protection. Of course, I won't be commenting on that. "I play football. We're playing in the divisional playoff game this Sunday against Los Angeles."

"So, it's a big game?" She takes another drink, giving a slight shrug of her shoulders. "Sorry, I don't really follow sports so I'm kind of clueless here."

I smile, actually a bit relieved to know that I'm with a girl who has absolutely no idea who I am, as opposed to some super fan trying to get in my pants. "Yeah, it's a big game."

"So, what team do you play for?"

"New England." I state proudly, but feel the need to say more when her expression remains completely blank. "The Patriots." She shrugs again, a small frown pulling at her mouth, so I say more. "We've won the Super Bowl championship several times over the last few years."

"Oh, that must have been exciting." She sort of perks up when she responds this time, but it's obvious she has absolutely no idea who I am, let alone anything about football. "What do you do on the team?"

I could tell her. I could. But it's clear she won't have a clue what I do, even if I do explain my position on the team, so I shift things back to her. "What about you Megan? What are you doing here in La La Land?"

She finishes the last of the champagne in her glass, and I motion to Jim for a refill, which he does promptly. "Would you two like dinner menus?"

We both nod yes, and she turns back to me. "I'm training some physicians on a new software my company is implementing at the UCLA Medical Center." She rolls her eyes and laughs. "I know, pretty tame compared to what you do."

I give her a once over this time, her brows furrowing as she looks down at herself to see what I'm looking at. Before she can ask, I joke. "I was wondering where you were hiding your pocket protector. Sounds like I've got a brainy pants in my midst."

"Well, I *can* play a mean game of chess." She grins back at me. "But I'm proud to say, I haven't let that impact my fashion choices."

"From what I've seen so far, anything you're wearing looks good on you." I watch as her cheeks flush a light pink, her fingers reaching out to play with the end of her braid, her gaze trailing slowly up my torso to my face.

"The same could be said about you." A coy smile dances across her lips as she takes another drink, her gaze on mine before she turns to focus on the menu in front of her. "Should we order something to eat?"

I wasn't sure at first, but after the look she just gave me, I think she's as attracted to me as much as I am to her. I know what I'd like to have for dinner, but I'm not sure if it's on the menu. "Something to eat sounds great."

We order from Jim, then continue talking, sharing details about ourselves as we get to know each other better. I find out she grew up in Connecticut, is an only child but has a best friend, Leah, who she loves like a sister. They met in college and now share an apartment together in New York City. Her dad died when she was twenty, but her mom is alive and still lives in the house she grew up in. She never got her license and still doesn't know how to drive, which makes Leah crazy whenever they go anywhere outside the city. In school she swam and rowed crew, so is definitely athletic, but, as demonstrated earlier, knows absolutely nothing about football.

And here's what I learned by just watching her. She ordered a chef salad, which came with each of the ingredients displayed in perfect rows over the lettuce. After she poured the dressing, she mixed everything together, then proceeded to pick each ingredient out individually and eat it one at a time. It wasn't until her third glass of champagne that she seemed to completely relax and look me in the eye each time she spoke. And every time she did speak, she waved her hands in the air, adding a dramatic flair to every story she told. She swipes her tongue across her lower lip each time she takes a drink of her champagne, drawing my attention perpetually to her divine mouth, which I've come to want against my own more than anything.

"Oh my God." Her hand slaps over the lips I'm craving, her eyes latching onto mine as they widen. A short puff of laughter escapes between her fingers as she lowers them. "I'm so sorry! All I've done is talk about myself. You must think I'm the most self-centered person ever."

I lean forward, sliding my hand over hers until our fingers entwine, hers still warm from her breath. "Don't apologize. It's a nice change of pace." And it really is. It's hard to go to many places now without being recognized, and when I do, I'm usually cornered and bombarded with questions. It was refreshing to have a conversation with someone and get to know them on an authentic level. I love listening to stories about someone else for once.

"No." She protests. "I want to know about you too." Her fingers squeeze mine in a gentle plea. "It's your turn. Tell me about you."

So I do. I tell her about growing up right here in Southern California with an older brother and a younger sister, and about my mom and dad. Somehow she gets me to tell her about my first girlfriend, who was also my first heart break, but then just as quickly, has me smiling again when I tell her how I helped my high school win its very first state championship football game ever. Of course, I have to explain to her how important football is to me and my dad so she can understand what that means, but I think she gets it.

After spilling my guts, I sit back, running a hand over my beard to smooth it down. It's definitely bushier than I'd like. She must sense my disdain, because her next question is about it.

"What's with the beard?" She waves a hand in the air when my brow shoots up at her bluntness. "Not that I mind it." I'm momentarily surprised when her fingers reach out and skim over my cheek and then down the beard. "It's softer than I would have thought." I smile as she continues. "I just wouldn't think it would be comfortable when you're wearing a helmet." Her eyes move to mine. "And hot as hell."

I let out a short laugh, because she has no idea how hot and itchy it gets when I'm playing. "Yep, it can be." I drag my fingers down the length of the growth. "It's a superstition kind of thing." She sips from her glass, listening intently as I try and explain. "It started a couple years ago.

It's a routine kind of thing. I started out not shaving for a game or two, and played really well. Then the whole team played well. And we were winning, and kept winning. You keep doing whatever you did before the game to keep whatever energy there is behind it going. So, no shaving. And now here I am, with this." I tug at the end of the beard as I shrug.

"So, where's the rest of the team tonight?" She leans into the back of the stool, my eyes zeroing in on the curve of her breasts as her back arches, my dick jerking to life again.

I lean forward in an attempt to hide my growing arousal from her, but I think she notices when her eyes bulge slightly after a glance in the direction of my waist, her cheeks flushing as her gaze darts back to her glass. I'm not sure if I should apologize, or compliment her for how my body is reacting to her, but the last thing I want to do is make her more uncomfortable, so I stick to a safer subject and answer her question. "Most of them are probably in their room." I motion to Jim again when I notice her glass is empty, and continue talking as he empties the last of the bottle into her flute. "We actually have a curfew."

"Seriously?" She says, a little too surprised. "I've almost drank this whole bottle." She smacks a hand over her face. "You must think I'm a lush."

"Definitely not what I'm thinking." I admit, not hiding my attraction as I lower my voice.

Her hand slides down her face in slow motion, her eyes lifting until they lock onto mine. Neither of us say anything as we stare at each other, our silent intensity fueling the desire that's been building between us all evening. The tip of her tongue, shiny and pink, pulls my attention toward her mouth as it sweeps over her bottom lip for the twentieth time tonight, a jolt shooting straight to my cock when she speaks. "Maybe you should walk me to my room before you break curfew then."

Chapter Three

Oh my God, oh my God, oh my God! I can't believe I just said that out loud to him. I think he might be slightly shocked too, based on how quickly he just threw his credit card at Jim when he brought the bill. I don't do things like this. I don't ask men back to my room. *EVER.* But good lord, this man is so damn hot, and sexy, and every wet dream I've ever had, so I honestly don't care. The hell with principles right now. I want this man, more than I can remember ever wanting anyone.

Every single time he took a sip of his water, or adjusted the chunky, expensive looking watch on his wrist, or motioned to Jim, I could not stop looking at his forearms. His finely corded and tanned forearms, the muscles shifting each time he moved, drawing me in like a bee to a flower dripping with pollen. I don't know why, but it turns me the hell on. Wondering what those hands could do to me.

Seeing the strength they obviously have. Good lord, I wish I had worn panties under my jeans instead of going commando. I'm so afraid my arousal for him is going to become obvious pretty soon.

He scribbles his signature on the bill, leaving a huge tip for Jim, which scores him bonus points. He stands, extending his hand to help me off my stool. I slip my hand into his, the strength of his fingers surrounding mine as they close possessively. I sway as I rise, not sure if it's from the champagne or from being this close to him, but my other hand lands on his chest to steady myself. *Whoa. Hard as a damn rock.*

"You okay?" His caramel eyes meeting mine with concern.

"Yes." I assure him, my hand reluctantly lifting off him to demonstrate how okay I am. "Think that last glass of champagne went right to my head."

"Then I definitely need to make sure you get to your room safely." His hand pulls at mine as he begins to walk toward the exit. I follow, willingly, my body drawn to his like a magnet as my shoulder leans against his. It's the first time I notice how good he smells. I close my eyes and inhale, hoping the singular sense of smell will enhance the pleasure of his scent. I savor the spicy aroma floating from him and let out a hum of approval. My eyes flutter open to find his face turned to mine, a crooked smile on his face.

"Did I just do that out loud?" I giggle trying to hide my embarrassment, then explain, my voice lowering an octave. "You smell amazing."

The elevator dings, and the doors slide open. We wait a couple seconds as a few people step out, and then we step inside, him looking over at me. "What floor?"

"Twenty-three." I breathe out, my heart racing as I realize I'm really doing this as he presses the button. The door slides closed with a soft clunk, and before I can blink, his hands move to my waist to turn and push me up against the wall. His entire body hovers an inch from mine, the heat of it radiating against mine as his face looms over me. My eyes trail to his mouth, his bottom lip wet from the swipe his tongue just made, my own bottom lip caught between my teeth.

"Look at me." His voice is husky and deep. My eyes shoot up to his. "I need to know you want this. That it's not the alcohol speaking." A hot breath flares from his nostrils before he continues. "Cause Lord knows no matter how badly I want you, I won't take advantage of you."

I surge forward, closing the distance between us as I fuse my mouth against his, his body tense for less than a second before his grip on my waist relaxes. One hand trails up my body to wrap around the back of my neck as he deepens our kiss, his tongue pushing against the seam of my lips until I open wide, my hands fisting the material of his shirt as I cling to pull him closer. His body crushes against mine, and I feel every defined inch of him as he molds to me. *Holy shit.*

I push him away abruptly, panting as our eyes meet. "I want this." I tilt to press an insistent kiss against his mouth. "I want you."

As if on cue, the elevator slides to a stop with a ding and

the doors open. He doesn't hesitate. He grabs my hand to lead me out of the elevator, looking at me for direction.

"Room 2380." I point. "It's the very last door on the left side." I use my free hand to fish my room key out of the back pocket of my jeans as we walk down the hall, swiping it over the sensor when we reach the door. Jasper pushes the handle down, shoving it open as he pulls me into the room, the door slamming behind us. The sound causes us both to freeze, our heads snapping in the direction of the loud noise, momentarily interrupting the urgency we felt only a second ago.

He turns, tugging my hand until I'm facing him, my breathing ragged as I look at him. "Last chance." He warns, taking a step, his chest grazing against the peaked nipples of my breasts, his fingers slowly winding the long length of my braid around his hand. "Tell me to leave now or I won't be able to."

"Stay." It's one word. It's all he needs. He tugs my hair, jerking my head back to slam his lips over mine and I'm lost. Lost to his smell, his touch, his desire. It consumes me like nothing I've ever experienced before, causing any sense I may have had, to vanish. I clutch onto his muscled biceps, my nails digging into the hard flesh as his other hand snakes around my waist to haul my body against him. My mouth opens in a surprised gasp when I feel the length of his arousal against my stomach. His teeth nip my bottom lip, then trail lower, his hand tugging my braid as he slowly sucks his way to the curve of my neck.

My core pulses with need, and I wrap a leg around his, grinding against his thigh in search of some kind of friction.

My fingers slide to his lower back, wrenching at the hem of his shirt to drag it over his head. He wastes no time mimicking my action, my shirt landing on top of his two seconds later. In the brief time we're apart, my eyes drink in a chest so finely chiseled that they widen, my senses again momentarily stunned that someone's body could be this perfect. I open my mouth to say just that to him, but he silences me before I can, his tongue swiping across my lips before sucking them against his own.

His hands slide under my ass and I feel him lift, my legs on autopilot as they wrap around his waist. Our kissing is almost frantic, my fingers weaving through the short locks of his hair as he moves us further into the room, stopping when he reaches the bed. His hand is hot as it splays across my back, his strength obvious as he lowers me to the bed, his mouth releasing mine. His eyes lock with mine, then shift to trail down my body, his gaze so intense it feels like he's actually touching me.

I take advantage of the space between us to graze my fingers over his torso, marveling at the contradiction of the hard ridges lying beneath silky soft skin. I have the sudden urge to lick him, to see if he tastes as delicious as he looks, but don't get the chance. Any thoughts I have are obliterated when the heat of his mouth closing over my nipple registers in my brain, my eyes rolling back as my lips part in a moan. He flicks his tongue over my hard peak through the satin of my bra, his hand gripping my breast as his lips surround my nipple and suck hard, drawing another long moan from me. My pussy throbs in time to every pull he takes on my breast, my need for him becoming desperate as he unclasps the front hook, sliding the material away to expose my bare skin.

My nails loosen the grip they have on his head to skim down his back until they find the waistband of his jeans, then continue until I reach the front. I tear at the button until it pops, shoving my hands inside, my fingers finding and wrapping around his girth. I squeeze when I feel his cock jerk against my hand, his mouth popping off my nipple on a growl. His body lifts away from mine, both of our chests heaving as our eyes meet, my grip tightening to keep him from drifting further away.

He glances down between our bodies, then back up at me, a slight grin lifting one corner of his mouth. "Don't worry, I'm not going anywhere."

My fingers relax, but instead of releasing him, I move to cup his cock in my palm. "I know right where I want you to go." I circle my fingers around him, pulling him toward my center to make sure my message is clear.

He pushes his hard length against my core, my hand stuck between us, his eyes dilating as he continues to stare at me. I clench my eyes breaking the contact when he rocks forward, the pressure against my clit sending a wave of pleasure crashing like a tidal wave over my entire body, his name rolling off my lips in a guttural moan. His body lifts off mine again, my eyes darting to his waist as he moves my hand away, then sigh in relief when he pushes his jeans and boxers down his legs. I shift, propping myself up slightly on my elbows so I can see all of him, and marvel again at how unbelievably beautiful his body is. My fingers twitch under me, the desire to trail them over every inch of his flesh causing my mouth to water.

"Your turn." His comment startles me out of my trance as he stands over me, his fingers working to release the button of my jeans, then pulling at the denim, his body stilling when they slide past my waist. "You're not wearing any underwear?" His gaze, on fire now, finds mine.

I snag my bottom lip between my teeth, shaking my head.

"Holy shit." He yanks my pants completely off, then moves his body over mine. "That's so god damn hot." His mouth crashes into mine, his tongue plunging inside to massage against my tongue, his hunger for me prodding between my legs as he lowers against me.

I widen my legs, spreading my knees so his entire body can fit between me, shuddering when his length rubs along the wet seam of my center. I shift my hips, shoving my pussy against his cock, trying to force him inside of me, the ridge of his crown sliding roughly over my clit, my body jerking from the contact. I snake a hand between our bodies, my fingers gliding around the wetness that's spread over his cock, and tug him toward my center. I can't remember ever needing someone as badly as I do in this moment, and let out a frustrated cry when I feel him tug his hips back.

"Condom?" He asks raggedly, his chest rising and falling quickly as he peers down at me.

"I'm on the pill." I slide my hand up and down his length, wanting to feel his smooth, hot skin inside of me, and not the latex of a condom. I've never had sex without a condom before, but for some reason, with him, it's all I want. I should ask him if he's clean. But for some reason I just know he is. I don't even need to ask the question. I tighten my grip to draw him to my center again.

"Are you sure?" The weight of his body welcome against mine as the tip of his cock nudges against the slit of my opening.

"Yes." I beg, spreading even wider, pressing my feet into the mattress as I shove my hips up, my opening spreading around his cock as he edges it in.

"Fuck." It comes out on a growl as his hips drive forward and slam into mine, his cock plunging inside of me. The muscles of my pussy contract around him, holding him tight as our bodies fuse together in perfect harmony. That fusion may have lasted a second, or maybe ten, I'm not sure, only coming back to earth when he begins to slowly pump in and out of me.

"So tight." He grunts as he thrusts his hips against me, his mouth capturing mine in a passion-filled kiss. His lips move against mine in a whisper, "Tell me what you need." He kisses me hard again, before moving against them to whisper again. "I want to make you come."

My pussy contracts around him as the breath of his words reach my ears. This man is perfection. "Don't stop." My fingers claw into the skin of his back as I lift my groin up to meet his. "Just don't stop Jasper."

"Not stopping." He pants into my mouth, his hips swiveling as he continues to pump in and out of me, his cock sliding against my clit each time he bears down, every nerve in my body starting to coil. Less than a minute later, the muscles in my pussy clench as fireworks explode behind my closed lids, and I moan in ecstasy, "yes, yes, yes…" Just as my muscles being to pulse, Jasper's body heaves into mine a final time, his cock thrusting hard as he growls out my name, his cum hot as he buries himself deep inside of me.

Chapter Four
_____

"Sorry." I murmur into her hair as I roll off her, pulling her against me, her head coming to rest in the crook of my arm. My heart is pounding against my rib cage like a prisoner trying to escape its cell, and I wonder if she can feel it. I didn't mean to practically attack her when we walked into the room, but something ignited in me from the very second I saw this woman. Or, more appropriately, ran in to her. From the moment my hand wrapped around her waist, before I even saw her face, some kind of electric charge surged through me. Since then it's been like a magnetic force calling me to her, and I knew I wouldn't feel complete until I was connected to her again.

"Sorry?" Her face lifts off my arm as she turns to look at me, her brow furrowed. "For what exactly? A great dinner, the company, or that amazing orgasm?"

An involuntary smile pulls at my mouth. "It wasn't exactly my best work." I run a hand over my face in attempt to hide my embarrassment. "The moment usually lasts more than five damn minutes."

"Best damn five minutes I've had in longer than I can remember" She chuffs out, laughing as she settles back into my shoulder. "But if you're saying it gets better, as soon as you're ready, I'm more than happy to let you prove it."

I put my hand over hers, which is drifting in a slow circle over my heart, and drag it down my body and over my groin. A quick gasp of breath spills over my chest when her fingers settle over my length, long and hard under her soft touch. Her hand relaxes at the base of my cock, and then strokes from root to tip, her touch light as a feather. I jerk in reaction against her palm, a groan of approval rumbling through my chest. Using the arm I have wrapped around her, I pull her further into me, her leg moving to drape over mine as she leans across my chest to look up at me. "I see you're up to the challenge?"

"I am if you are." I chuckle, tilting forward to brush my lips against hers, the need to taste her mouth against mine all consuming. She leans away from me before I can deepen the kiss, her hand moving from my throbbing cock to my hip, using it as leverage as she moves to stand. I sit up, wondering if I pushed too fast, but before I can ask, she speaks.

"Hold that thought." She's adorable as she tries to hide her naked body by crossing her arms, her cheeks flushing the tell-tale sign of pink in embarrassment. "I really need to use the bathroom and maybe just freshen things up a little bit."

"Of course." I let out the breath I was holding in relief and smile up at her. "Take your time."

She starts padding in the direction of a door that I assume is the bathroom, but then stops and twists her head back to me. "Don't leave."

I shake my head once. "I won't."

She nods, turning back in the direction she's walking, my eyes glued to her ass. An ass that's shaped like a damn upside down heart, complete with dimples on her lower back. My gaze swings up when I see her shift around again in the entrance to the bathroom, her arm extending to point to a mini-fridge under the large, flat-screen television across from the bed. "There's water if you want it." Then she disappears, closing the door behind her.

I glance at the clock next to the bed. 9:27. *Shit*. I should really throw my clothes back on, thank her for a great time, and get the hell back to my room. I've got a ten o'clock curfew and practice in less than twelve hours from now. For one of the biggest games of my career. I stand, looking down at my dick, still hard as a fucking rock, and see it's abundantly clear how it feels about leaving. Damn it. I don't want to leave either. Yeah, the sex, even though only five minutes, was incredible. I'd be lying if I didn't admit I wanted more, but I also really like this girl. There is something different happening with her. A connection so natural, so easy, that it just feels like it's meant to be.

Screw it. I pick my jeans up from the floor and fish my cell out of the front pocket. I bring up a text window and type in a message to Doug, my teammate, and also my roommate here at the hotel.

Cover for me? Be back late.

Less than three seconds later, dots start dancing on the screen as he types a reply. I roll my eyes when I see his response.

It's your ass. Hope hers is worth it.

That's his way of agreeing. It would be too easy to just say sure. It's a guy thing. We can't do anything straight forward if it involves any kind of feelings. I set the phone on the table next to the bed, then grab a bottle of water from the mini-fridge she pointed to. I look around the room, noting a laptop computer on the desk, a pile of paperwork next to it, and a black bag slung over the chair. They are the only personal items on display in the room, everything else is put away somewhere. She's either neat as a mouse, or packs extremely light. Before I can investigate further, the door to the bathroom opens, and she appears, her body wrapped in a short, silk robe in a yellow and gray floral pattern. She covered up, and I immediately wonder if that means she's changed her mind about round two, and in the next moment, makes me hyper aware of how naked I still am.

"Sorry." I place the water on the side table, then bend over to grab my jeans. Her hand is over mine before I can stand to put them on.

"What are you doing?" Her voice is soft, but there's an obvious nervous edge lacing the question.

I straighten, lifting my eyes, then raise my shoulders in a slight shrug. "I thought maybe you wanted me to leave."

One side of her mouth quirks up in a coy smile as she shakes her head back and forth, her gaze staying locked on mine. "Nope." Her hand presses flat against the center of my chest, and with a strength that surprises me, shoves me back onto the bed. "Definitely do not want that." My brows shoot up when she climbs up on the bed next to me, one leg lifting over me as she straddles my waist, her robe parting around her legs as she hovers over me. "I mean, unless you want to." She tilts her head, watching my reaction as the heat of her core comes to rest on my hard length as her hips settle on mine.

"Nope." I slide my hands up her bare thighs, stopping when I reach the lacey edging of her robe. "Not what I want at all."

"Good." Her hands land gently on the top of my chest. "Because five minutes was definitely not enough." Her fingers begin to move over my skin, tracing over the ridges of muscle defining my torso, my eyes following their path until she speaks again. "Your body is…" She looks down at me, her teeth capturing her lower lip, the surface shiny when she releases it to continue talking. "It's perfection." Her fingers continue to explore, skimming over the raised veins cording my forearms. "Is it weird that I think your arms may be the sexiest things I've ever seen?" She laughs, her core vibrating against me, my cock jerking along her heat, stifling her instantly, her eyes widening as they jump to mine.

"No stranger than my wanting to unbraid your hair." I stare up at her, then shift my body so that I'm sitting, her legs sliding around my waist as we come face-to-face.

"You want to unbraid my hair?" She murmurs, her lips only inches from mine.

"Uh-huh." I close the distance between us, pressing my mouth to hers, my fingers moving at the same time to remove the elastic binding the end of her hair. I pull back from her mouth, the material of her robe, cool and smooth against my chest as our bodies remain connected. "I want to see it loose." I begin unthreading her hair, silencing any objection she might have with a swipe of my tongue against her parted smile. Her hands glide around my neck, her nails digging into the base of my scalp as I devour the taste of her. She squashes her body to mine as I continue inching up the length of her braid, dragging my fingers through each crossed section, until all of her hair flows freely down her back.

I fist a handful of the soft locks, and yank gently, her mouth forming a small O shape as a short yelp of surprise escapes. I tug again, exposing more of her neck, the top of her robe sliding open to release her breasts as her back arches. A waterfall of kinky waves cascade down behind her, brushing against my thighs as I drop my mouth against her neck. I skim my lips over her delicate skin, leaving a trail of wet kisses in my wake as I descend lower, the taste of her salty and sweet against my tongue. I release the grip I have on her tresses to slide my hand down her back, then splay it wide between her shoulder blades to hold her in place as I wrap my lips around one exposed nipple.

Her body jolts, a low moan filling the air, the vibration of it tingling against my mouth, my free hand moving over her other breast, her nipple taut and hard against the palm of my hand. I suck hard on the nipple caught between my teeth, pinching the other one between my fingers, my cock growing even harder against her. She groans out my name, her legs locking around me as she presses her center into my throbbing dick. My teeth bite around the hard peak of the nipple I was flicking against my tongue, a growl ripping from me as I buck my hips up into hers. Her fingernails scrape from my shoulders to the center of my back as she shifts her hips to slide up and then down my aching length, my name, low and breathy, puffing from her mouth. I lave my tongue over the tip of her breast, softening the edge of the bite, then suck again, my lips curving up when she yells my name out again. Nothing has ever sounded sweeter. I want to talk to her. Tell her she's so damn beautiful. Ask her if she wants more. But before I can, she pulls back from me abruptly, a small pop sounding as her breast leaves the suction of my mouth. I snap my eyes to hers, my chest rising and falling sharply as I speak. "What's wrong?"

She shakes her head, scooting her body down to the top of my thighs before rising up on her knees. She pulls at the tie on her rob, then slides it completely off, dropping it to the floor, leaving her naked over me. "Absolutely nothing." Her attention shifts down to my waist, her tongue darting out between her parted lips, sweeping over them as her gaze drags slowly up my torso until she's looking me in the eye again. "I just thought we wanted this to last more than five minutes." She leans over me, planting her hands on each of my shoulders, then lowers her face, brushing wet lips against mine. Her lashes lift as she peeks up at me, her voice thick with lust when she speaks. "And, I want to taste you."

I snag a hand around the back of her head and crush my

mouth against hers in a kiss so hard it borders on brutal. I force my tongue between her lips, trying to lose myself in her taste so I don't slam inside her pussy instead. When I've claimed every inch of her mouth, I tear myself away, my breath panting against her swollen lips, the thought of them around my shaft sending a shock right to my groin. "Are you sure?"

Her tongue snakes out between her lips, the pink tip swiping over my mouth in one long stroke before she leans back, bobbing her head once. "Oh, I'm sure." I practically come right then, my cock thumping against my waist in anticipation when her body slides further down my legs. I fall back against the bed, my fingers threading into her downy mane as her head dips under my chin, just below my beard. Hungry lips press against the base of my throat, turning into small nips as she descends lower, my feet digging into the mattress when her tongue slides lazily over my nipple. Her mouth closes around the flat disk surrounding my sensitive peak, the wet heat causing my flesh to prick into a thousand tiny bumps, my grip on her hair tightening when she sucks, drawing out a moan from deep inside me.

She scrapes her teeth over my nipple, then covers it again with her entire mouth, sucking it roughly. The hand I have on her head tightens, pushing her mouth even harder onto my nipple, my hips pumping in search of her. My other hand somehow manages to find its way between her legs, and I slide my fingers against her pussy, groaning loudly when I feel how wet she is. Her mouth opens in a moan when I plunge two digits into her opening, the attention to my nipple forgotten as she grinds down onto my hand. I pump them in and out of her, her hair fanning out across my chest when her cheek drops against it, her fingers digging into my shoulders as she lets out a moan. "Not fair."

"All's fair in love and war, baby." I chuckle, using my thumb to push against her clit, eliciting another moan from her. As much as I want to feel her mouth around my cock, I want inside of her pussy even more. I drag my fingers out of her hair to grab around the base of my cock, squeezing it as I lift it off my stomach. She seems to understand what I want without my actually saying it, her body shifting so that it's over me, my fingers sliding out of her to guide her center over mine. I tighten the grip on my cock, holding it firm as her heat starts to surround me, letting go when I feel her core brush up against my knuckles. As soon as my hand is free, her hips are against mine, my cock burying deep inside her. We groan out our combined relief, stilling for only a second before her hips glide forward as she begins to rock. She shifts, sitting up straighter, her hair flying over her shoulder as she tosses her head back, her hands planting on my chest as she grinds deeper with each slide of her hips.

I dig my fingers into the tops of her thighs, forcing her up and down the entire length of my cock, making sure her clit drags against the edge of my crown, her hips bucking every single time. I know she's going to come before she does. Her fingers curl, her short nails breaking the skin on my chest as the muscles in her body begin to contract, the skin around her nipples puckering as they grow harder, the walls of her pussy clenching around my cock in a slow grip. I wait until she explodes, my name tumbling from her mouth as she falls over the edge, then flip her in one smooth motion, driving my cock as deep as it can go.

I smash my mouth over hers when her eyes fly open, capturing her cry of surprise with my lips. I continue pumping into her, her core pulsing wildly around me as I do, inducing a state of arousal I've never experienced before. My cock feels longer, harder, fucking better than it's ever felt as I plunge deeper and deeper inside of her. My body tenses tight then erupts, both of us crying out, clinging to the other in an attempt to get closer as my warm cum spurts inside of her on one last, jutting stroke. White specks of light flash against the back of my eyelids, my body floating somewhere in space as my brain simply stops working as I hum with pleasure.

When the last pulse of our mating throbs between us, I pull gently out, and then collapse beside her. She rolls onto her side, so I curl myself around her, pulling her back flush to my front, noticing she's a perfect fit. I place my hand over hers and lace our fingers together. I can feel the rapid drumming of her heart through her chest where our hands rest. "Are you okay?"

"Uh-huh." She murmurs, her body relaxing into mine as she scoots further into me. "Just need a minute."

I tighten my hold around her, my body softening against hers, my nose buried in the coconut scent of her sun-colored hair, the last thing I remember before waking up three hours later.

Chapter Five

I jerk awake, my lids flying open as I spring into a sitting position, a blanket sliding down to my waist. I do a quick scan of the room, and determine its empty except for me. At first, relief sweeps through me, but then, only a second later, disappointment. I glance at the clock next to the bed, surprised that it's almost seven. I slept through the entire night, Jasper having snuck out sometime during that time. I'm still on top of the quilt covering the bed. It dawns on me that he found a blanket somewhere in the room to cover me with before he left, and that at least makes me feel a little better. I pull it over my body as I lay back down on the bed.

I close my eyes, slapping a hand over my face as I blow out a heavy breath. What in the world possessed me last night? I truly must have lost my ever-loving-mind to bring an almost complete stranger back to my room, and then have sex with him. Not once, but TWICE. Granted, he was absolutely delicious in every sense of the word, and God help me, so was the sex. But seriously, this is not something I do. But damn, I'd do it again right now if he was still here. And I'd be lying to myself if I didn't admit that much. I shake my head, pulling my hand away to sit up again when I hear my cell alert me of a text.

I look in the direction of the pinging noise, and realize my phone is in the back pocket of the jeans I was wearing last night. Still lying in a heap on the floor where Jasper tossed them after stripping them off of me. My core clenches as I recall the feel of his body against mine, and I throw the covers off me as I leap up from the bed. I will not let myself get sucked down this rabbit hole. Last night was amazing, and something I definitely don't regret, but it's over.

I snatch my jeans off the floor, my phone thumping to the carpet as it slides out of the pocket, and I mumble in frustration as I lean over to grab it. I smile when I see Leah's name on the screen, remembering its three hours ahead in New York and that she's actually up. Before I respond, I use the bathroom, then find my robe, wrapping it around me as I plop back down on the bed. I know she's probably in the office, but take a chance, and try calling instead of texting, in case she can actually talk.

"Did I wake you up?" Her voice, hushed slightly, asks over the phone.

"No, I was up." I scoot further back on the bed. "Can you talk, or are you busy, busy, busy?"

"Do you need to talk?" I love that she can read me like a book. "I'm at my desk, but I can go down to the lobby and grab a coffee."

I nod my head, even though I know she can't see me. "Yes, definitely need to talk."

"Ooooh." She draws out. "Now I'm curious."

"Just call me back when you're in the lobby." I end the call before she can interrogate me further, letting myself fall back onto the bed, my head hitting the pillow. I turn my head, inhaling deeply as I do, Jasper's spicy scent filling my nostrils. This must be the pillow he used. I raise my head, lifting my arms under my head at same time to yank the pillow out, then hug it to my chest. I drop my face into the soft cotton fabric, practically snorting it up my nose I sniff so hard, my body warming in response to his smell. I let out a long hum of appreciation, squeezing tightly, wishing it was him in my arms instead, then burst out laughing, my face still buried. I'm seriously losing it over this man!

My phone rings, interrupting my self-admonishment abruptly as I fling the pillow off my face to reach blindly to find my phone. My fingers locate and wrap around the insistent device, and I raise it to my ear. I realize she's Facetiming me, so angle the phone over my face as I press accept. She appears a second later, her brows knit together as she frowns at me with concern. "You haven't showered yet?"

"It's barely seven here." I defend, noticing the weather behind the large, plate-glass window she's sitting in front of. "It's still snowing?"

"Ugh." Her head turns to look outside, then back at me through the phone. "Yes, for hours now. Getting to the office this morning was a nightmare. Thank God for the subway."

"Well, not to make you too jealous, but it was in the seventies here yesterday." I grin widely when her mouth drops open.

"So not fair." She takes a sip of whatever she's drinking, most likely a mocha cappuccino, then gives me a serious look. "Talk to me. I've only got ten minutes. Did you meet some hot doctor from the hospital and finally get laid?"

"He wasn't a doctor." I scrunch my eyes closed, afraid to see what her reaction's going to be, not that it matters, because the loud screech coming through the phone makes it clear.

"You slut!" She giggles. "Tell me everything!"

I open my eyes, and blow out a breath. "Leah, I couldn't even help myself." I shake my head, splaying a hand across my face, my fingers spread wide so I can peek at her through them as I continue. "He was that frickin' fine. And Lord help me, so was the sex."

"Oh my God. You little minx! Tell me all the details. I want to know everything." She squeals, hopping up and down in her seat.

"I met him here at the hotel, yesterday, kind of by accident." The hand that was on my face is now waving in the air as I recount what happened in the lobby yesterday, then about how he found me in the bar, and finally, how we somehow ended up making out in the elevator. "Leah, that first kiss. If I actually had panties on, they would have burst into flames it was that scorching hot."

"Please tell me you did it in his room and not on the elevator." She chuckles, her head tilting as one brow shoots up in her weak attempt to chastise me.

"He's got a roommate, but don't worry, we went to my room."

"Wait, a roommate?" Her tone growing serious. "Please don't tell me you hooked up with some college guy on winter break or something."

"Nope." My mouth breaks into a wide smile as I shake my head. "He's a professional football player."

"Shut the fuck up!" She yells, her hand slamming over her mouth as her eyes pop wide. Her hand lowers a second later as she shifts her attention to apologize to someone that must be standing near her, then swings quickly back to me, her voice softer. "A professional athlete?" She throws her head back as she lets out a hearty laugh, then looks back at me. "Only you. Guess I don't have to ask how his endurance was?" I feel my face heat as I remember just how good his *endurance* was, Leah's mouth dropping open before speaking again when she registers my reaction. "I hate you so much right now." She smiles as she rolls her eyes. "But only because I'm green with jealousy."

"Well, don't be." I shrug, trying to appear nonchalant, even though it's not how I'm really feeling. "He snuck out sometime during the night while I was sleeping. No note or anything."

"Seriously?" Her tone sharp. "What's his name? What team does he play for? I'm going to ask Tom about him." Tom is her older brother, and knows everything there is to possibly know about football. He played in high school, played in college, and was drafted to the NFL. Unfortunately, he never got to play professionally due to a debilitating knee injury he suffered in a car accident only a month before he was supposed to start.

"No, absolutely not!" I declare. "Tom will never let me live it down if he knows I hooked up with some football player." Especially since I had a mad crush on him my entire sophomore year of college. I met him the summer between my freshman and sophomore year when I spent half the break at Leah's house. There was a lot of flirting and one stolen kiss, and then the car accident. Any hopes or dreams I had of more between us were squashed when his whole world collapsed. I had long since moved on, but I still didn't want him being privy to my one-night-stand.

"Pffft, I'm sure he could care less." Leah never knew the extent of the crush I had on her older brother. Sometimes, some things just stay hidden no matter how close friends are. "I'm just going to ask him about the guy. I won't say a thing about why. I promise!"

"Argh!" I gripe out, knowing I've told her enough now that she won't give up easily. "Fine. His name is Jasper Chase."

"From the Patriots?" Her brows fly high when her eyes grow large.

I nod, my heart rate picking up a notch at her response.

"Jesus, Meg, even I know who Jasper Chase is." She gives me a dramatic eye roll, and repeats her earlier sentiment. "Only you."

"What's that supposed to mean?" I pout.

"He's only one of the most popular wide receivers in the league, and girl, definitely one of the hottest. The fact that you have no clue at all about this is just so you."

I sit up on the bed, shrugging my shoulders as I do. "I can't help it if I don't like football."

"Well, you sure know how to pick 'em, I'll give you that." She laughs shaking her head. "Babe, I gotta go. It's been way more than ten minutes, and you know what happens if the wicked witch comes looking for me and I'm not at my desk." The wicked witch is her boss in the marketing firm she works for, and has earned her name due to her evil temper.

"Okay, go. I need to jump in the shower anyway. I have to be at the hospital by nine." I slide off the bed to stand.

"Yeah, go wash that dirty sex off yourself, you nasty thing." She teases, laughing.

I stick my tongue out at her, clicking end before she can respond, then head to the bathroom.

I walk back into the hotel just after three, noting that it's much quieter, and empty, than it was the previous day. I'm secretly hoping Jasper might be waiting for me, but am still surprised when a wave of disappoint crashes over me when he's not. I shake off the feeling, squaring my shoulders as I force myself to stand straighter as I walk across the lobby to the elevators.

"Oh, Ms. Lewis!" I stop short hearing my name called out from one of the people standing behind the registration counter. "I'm so glad I saw you."

I change my direction to head that way instead, stopping when I reach the young woman. "Yes, is there a problem?"

Maybe there was a noise complaint last night from whomever was stuck on the other side of the wall from my room. Jasper and I weren't exactly quiet.

"Oh no, not at all." The woman, who's wearing a name tag displaying Jennifer, reassures me with a smile. "I just wanted to let you know that there was a delivery for you, and that I had it brought to your room."

"A delivery?" I repeat, racking my brain as I try and remember if the New York office was going to send something to me.

"Yes ma'am." She's beaming at me, wearing a smile that seems to be trying to tell me something. Unbeknownst to her, I'm not getting the message as I stare back at her with a blank expression.

"Okay." I state slowly, confusion dragging out my response. I thank her, then walk back in the direction of the elevator, boarding when the doors slide open. I press the button for my floor, exiting when I arrive, heading for my room. I dig for the key in my purse, yanking it out when I finally find it, then swipe it over the sensor, pushing the door open when it turns green. I step inside, halting in my tracks when I spot what's been delivered for me. A huge bouquet of pink roses is sitting on the desk in front of the window, a note attached.

I drop my bag to the floor, mindless of where it lands as I stride to the flowers, their scent filling the space in my small room. I cradle my hands around the bottom of the green circumference of the flowers, then bend, burying my nose in the soft petals to inhale deeply. I close my eyes, my lips curving into a wide smile as I savor the fragrance. When I pull back, I marvel at their simple beauty, my mouth gaping when I count and realize there are thirty roses in the vase. I shake my head in disbelief, then snag the card out of the holder in the middle of the arrangement. I tear the small envelope open carefully, my pulse quickening as I begin to read the print scrawled on the card.

> *Megan,*
> *Sorry I had to leave before you woke.*
> *Dinner again tonight?*
> *I'm free any time after four.*
> *Call me 508-476-8932.*
> *xo*
> *Jasper*

I admit it. It stung a little when I woke up this morning to not only find him gone, but also because he didn't leave a note or say goodbye. Even though I knew when I brought him back to my room, we were hooking up and a one night stand is a one night stand, I still expected some kind of closure. This however, made up for it completely.

I place the note on the table beside the vase, then scoot back over to my bag on the floor to find my phone. Once I locate it, I unlock the screen, find Leah's number and press call. She answers on the second ring. "Hey Meg."

"He sent me roses!" I blurt out, not even bothering to give her a proper greeting.

"What?" She bellows through the phone. "Talk louder! There was a train going by."

I realize she must be in the subway waiting for her train

home, so I raise my voice to accommodate for the background noise, repeating what I just said. "He sent me roses!"

"He did?" She lets out a short squeal. "So much better than a note!" There's a short pause, and I'm about to answer, but she interjects. "Did he send a card? What did it say? Does he love you already?"

"Shut up!" I respond on a laugh, rolling my eyes. "He wants to take me to dinner tonight."

"You mean, he's looking for round two?" The sarcasm in her tone doesn't go unnoticed.

"So what if he is? Leah, he's hot. I'm up for another round." I walk back over to the roses and brush my fingers over the delicate petals, wondering out loud. "Maybe I am a slut."

"You are so not a slut. Stop that." She admonishes.

"I mean, it's a really nice bouquet of roses. I should at least thank him." I mumble more to myself than to her.

"I can't hear you." She yells again. "Hold on, I'm getting on the train." I wait, taking the phone away from my ear long enough to snap and send her a picture of the flowers. "Okay, that's better. What did you say again?"

I can actually hear just her, and not a bunch of noise, so lower my voice. "Look at your texts. I just sent you a picture."

There's a moment of silence, then her response. "Holy crap. How many freaking roses did he send you?"

"Thirty." I plop down on the bed, chewing on a fingernail. "It's nice, right?"

"Um, more than nice. It's gorgeous."

"He left me his number."

"I can hear you chewing your nails through the phone." She chastises, the frown on her face evident through the tone in her voice as she continues. "Are you going to call him?"

"I mean, I have to at least say thank you for the roses, right?" I move my thumbnail to my mouth, then pull it away before I bite, shoving my hand under my leg.

"Yeah, but how nice of a thank you do you want to give him?" She snorts. "Did you pack anything dressy to wear, or just work stuff?"

I stand and walk to the closet, sliding the door open. Everything I packed was ironed and hung up as soon as I arrived. I'm a little OCD like that. I run my fingers along all the outfits, trying to determine if anything would be suitable. "I mean, I have a nice dress. And of course work outfits, but those are boring. And my comfy jeans."

"Which dress did you bring?" She demands, making it clear she's decided I'm going on the date.

"The black one." I reach for it to pull it free.

"That doesn't really narrow it down for me, Meg." She sighs dramatically. "You have about ten in your closet."

"The halter-top one. It's sleeveless and kind of has that short, flowy skirt." There's nothing but silence on the other end of the phone, so I continue giving her clues. "You know, the one I wore that time we went to that club where that band was playing and the drummer bought us those blue shots." A description only a best friend would understand.

"Oh, that dress!" She exclaims. "That's perfect! Wear that!"

"What if he takes me to a taco truck?" I joke, wondering if maybe it's too dressy for the L.A. scene.

"Then you'll be the hottest one there. Except for the hot sauce."

She laughs out loud at her own joke, and I can't help but join her. "You're so corny sometimes."

"I know, but it's why you love me." She counters.

"It's true. I do." I smile wide as I glance at the clock. "He said to call him after four, and it's just after three-thirty here. What time should I text him? I don't want to look too eager."

"You can give eager beaver a whole new meaning." She cracks up at her own joke again, stopping after a second when I don't respond. "Okay, sorry. I couldn't resist."

"Yeah, yeah." I shake my head, still smiling. "Seriously, how long should I wait til I call him?"

"You could make him squirm a little. I mean, he doesn't know how late you're working and anticipation always sweetens the reward." She clucks her tongue, a habit she has when she's thinking, then continues. "Or you could just text him now. Screw all the mind games."

"Winner." I declare. "I so don't want to play games."

"No. Just get laid again apparently." Leah teases. "But I mean, it's Jasper Fucking Chase. Girl, if you don't take him up on the offer, I'll hop on a plane right now."

"That won't be necessary." I assure her. "I think I've got this."

"Then go get him." She giggles. "And make sure you call me tomorrow! I want to know everything!"

"Okay, I will." I promise her, saying goodbye as I end

that call, so I can make another. I get up to retrieve the card, then create a new contact in my phone for Jasper, entering his number. I don't overthink it, well any more than I already have, and send him a text.

Hi, it's Megan. Would love to have dinner. Meet you in the lobby at six-thirty?

I'm surprised when my phone beeps only a minute later, my heart ricocheting against my chest as I read his text, unable to contain my excitement as I hop in place.

See you then. Can't wait.

Chapter Six

"I told you she would say yes." Doug states with supreme confidence from over my shoulder.

"What the fuck, dude?" I throw a harsh look behind me. "Stop reading my damn texts." I turn around so he can't see what I'm writing back to Megan, shielding my phone from his view until after I hit send. "A little privacy please?"

"I bet it was the roses." Doug continues, undeterred. "Chicks love when you send them flowers."

"It was my idea to send the roses, not yours asshole." I remind him.

"So, where you going to take her?" Still ignoring my defense in the role he played in setting up this date, he walks beside me as we leave the locker room. "Home to meet mom and dad?"

I stop in my tracks. "I met her last night man. Don't think we're quite there yet." I shake my head and start walking again. "I was thinking more along the lines of The Palm for a nice steak."

"Does she eat meat?" He bursts out laughing at the double meaning of his question, then stops abruptly when he sees the look I'm throwing his way. "I'm just saying, some of the girls these days are vegan or vegetarian or whatever the trend is."

"I've got it covered, thanks." I reach the bus back to the hotel and climb on board, finding a seat next to a window. I pull my headphones on, effectively ending any further conversation on the subject with Doug. I actually don't have much covered. I wasn't even sure Megan would want to see me again, so I hadn't thought about where to take her until Doug brought it up. I do like the Palm though.

I bring up a text session on my phone and draft a message to my personal assistant asking her if she can make a reservation at the Palm and secure a car service for me. She responds within seconds letting me know she'll take care of everything. Can't complain about having an assistant. Definitely takes the hassle out of everything for me. I'm about to close my eyes and relax for the rest of the ride, but snap to attention, thinking I should probably send Megan a text letting her know where I'm taking her. I know she's here on a business trip and have no idea if she's got the proper clothes for dinner out. Not that I didn't like her in the jeans she had on last night, especially with the commando game she was sporting. But I didn't want her to feel uncomfortable if I brought her some place she didn't have an outfit for. I may not know much, but I know this much from having a younger sister.

I bring up a new text window for her, type, delete, type and delete again, then finally send my last attempt to sound somewhat cool and aloof:

-Made reservations at The Palm for 7. Unless you want some place more casual?

I reread the message at least seven times after I send it, hoping it doesn't sound too pretentious, and start to worry when she doesn't text back right away. I crank up the music on my headphones, hoping to drown out some of the doubt ringing in my head. I practically jump out of my seat when the text alert sounds, my nerves coiled tight as a rattlesnake as I was trying to pretend I was being patient. I swipe my screen to read the message, smiling in relief when I see what she's written.

-The Palm sounds perfect. See you soon. Xo

When we get back to the hotel, I head right to my room. I'm in luck because Doug's going to watch game tapes with some of the other guys, so I've got the place to myself. All I want to do is take a nap before tonight. One, I'm tired as hell from practice today. Two, I only got about five hours of solid sleep last night. And three, I'm hoping I get even less tonight.

Last night was the first time in a really long time that I connected with a woman on a personal level. Which made our physical connection that much more intimate and intense, a definite bonus. Finding a woman to keep my bed warm hasn't been a problem since I was in college, but finding one I actually enjoyed being with was rare. I thought I had possibly found that with my last girlfriend, but the more time I spent with her, the more I came to realize she only showed me what was needed to keep her on my arm and in the spotlight. Megan barely realized who my damn team was, let alone me. Which was pretty damn nice. I wanted someone genuine and real without having to worry about whether or not they were interested in me, and not the fame that came from being around me.

I already took a shower back at the locker room, so I change into a pair of sweats and a t-shirt. I stare at my reflection in the bathroom mirror, my eyes focusing on the whiskers framing most of my lower face. I grasp a handful of the growth in my fingers, and contemplate shaving it for just a moment, then shake my head. I can't do it, even though there's a huge part of me that wants to. I'd like to show Megan the cleaner, smoother version of myself, and not the grizzly bear I've become with the beard, but superstition wins this decision hands down. I leave the bathroom, place a wake-up call, and then climb into the bed, falling asleep almost immediately.

It's six-twenty, and I'm pacing in the lobby, even though I'm early and have no reason to be nervous. I know she's going to show up, and I know without a doubt we'll have a good time because being with her is just easy. When a group of people flood into the lobby, I wander into a far corner of the space, wanting to stay out of the public eye in case I'm recognized. The last thing I want tonight is to be mobbed, especially when I'm with Megan. While it's flattering and I love my fans, it can be overwhelming when a hundred people or more surround you like a caged animal.

I'm facing the window, my back to the room as an extra ounce of protection against being recognized, but still feel it when she steps off the elevator and glides into the room. It's not the clicking of heels, or even her scent, but a current of energy that seems to find and pull me in her direction. I spin around, seeing her before she sees me, and I'm glad. I want this stolen moment to admire how stunning she looks. She's wearing a short black dress that gathers in a collar around her neck, leaving her arms exposed. Her legs are bare except for the swish of fabric against her upper thighs as she turns in a slow circle, black heels strapped to her feet, as she scans the room. What gets me though is her hair. She's left it down, and as she turns her back to me, I notice it falls almost to her waist. Its golden color shimmers like smooth silk in the soft lights of the lobby, causing everything below my waist to react as I remember how the strands felt across my naked chest the night before.

I shove my hands in the pockets of my pants in an attempt to hide the effect she has on me, then stride toward her. Her cheeks lift when she notices me, her smile lighting up her face, my own mouth breaking into a grin in response. She begins walking, closing the distance between us quickly as we meet in the middle. As if I'd done it a hundred times, my hand snakes around her waist to pull her close, my lips brushing against her cheek before I whisper in her ear. "You look beautiful."

She surprises me when instead of stepping away, leans into me, wrapping an arm around my shoulder to hug me, the hair vibrating against my neck when she hums in appreciation. "You smell so good."

I tighten my arm around her waist to mold her body into mine, her head under my nose. "So do you." At this rate, we're not even going to make it out of the hotel, never mind dinner. My dick throbs between us when her other hand slides under my suit jacket to grip onto the back of my shirt.

"Happy to see me?" She giggles, her breath warm on the skin of my neck.

"Extremely." I confess, the bulge in my pants a dead giveaway. I push back gently, taking the hand that's around my waist into my own. "And if we don't leave now, we won't be making it to dinner."

"As tempting as that sounds, I'm starving." Her eyes peek up at me from under her lashes, her cheeks flushing a light pink when she continues. "But I know what I want for dessert."

My cock jerks, and I shift, pulling her with me as I lead us to the exit of the lobby. "You might just be too good to be true." My voice a rough growl.

"I was thinking the exact same thing." She laughs, her body swaying into mine as we walk through the door. The car I ordered is waiting, the driver opening the back door as I steer her towards it. She turns her face to mine. "Is that for us?"

"Mr. Chase." The driver nods to me, then address us both, answering her question for me. "I'm Henry, and will be your driver for tonight."

"I guess that answers that." She smiles at me as I assist her into the seat. "Thank you."

Henry closes her door, and we both move to the other side of the vehicle, each opening our own doors before we settle into our respective seats. As I relax next to her, I slide my hand across the gap between us to her lap, entwining my fingers over hers, noticing how small and delicate her hand is compared to mine.

"The Palm, sir?" Henry asks from the front of the car as he pulls away from the hotel and into traffic.

"Please." I confirm, then turn my attention to Megan. "I know I already said it once, but you really do look beautiful."

"So do you. I mean--" Her eyes sweep over my body, crossing and uncrossing her legs as she shifts a little closer to me. "You look quite handsome."

I glance down at my frame covered in a dark suit, made more casual by wearing a fitted black sweater instead of a dress shirt, then laugh out loud as I realize we're both dressed entirely in black. "We look like we're going to a funeral instead of dinner."

"Oh my god, you're right!" Laughter spills from her parted smile as she nods. "It's the only non-worky thing I had with me, besides the jeans I wore last night, and I think those were a bit too casual."

"You're perfect." I assure her. "Black is always a fashion statement, right?"

"Can never go wrong with a little black dress." She shrugs, her expression turning more serious as her gaze meets mine. "Or thirty long-stemmed-roses." Her fingers squeeze lightly around mine. "Thank you for them. I don't think I've ever been more surprised or touched."

"It was my pleasure." I lift her hand to my mouth, pressing a kiss against the back of it before returning it to her lap. "Sorry I had to leave before you woke up."

"You really don't need to apologize. I know you had a curfew, and practice." She shifts her body a fraction closer to me, lowering her voice. "And you know, there were no expectations. We picked each other up in a bar. We had amazing sex. It is what it is."

I stare at her, not saying anything for a few moments as I think about how I want to reply to her statement. Yeah, we were strangers who picked each other up. Yeah, we had some pretty mind-blowing sex. And yeah, that usually is the scenario for a great one night stand. And I know I could have left it at that. But I also know I would have regretted it if I did. One night with her wasn't enough. I thought about her all day and wanted to know more about her. I wanted to know what her favorite color, television show, foods, drinks and places were. I wanted to know what made her laugh out loud, or what made her really angry. I wanted to know if she usually slept with her hair up, or did she leave it loose. And I really wanted to know if she sounded the same moaning my name in the morning, as she did at night. But telling her all this would surely have her sprinting in the other direction, so I keep silent.

She lets go of my hand to adjust the hem of her dress, her eyes darting out the window and away from me, and I realize I've paused a little too long. "One night with you definitely isn't enough."

Her eyes sweep back to mine, relief evident in the soft gaze of her indigo eyes as her fingers weave through mine once more. I use this connection to tug her body closer, tilting my head to close the remaining distance between us so I can slide my lips over hers. My other hand moves to cup her cheek, our kiss deepening as I angle her head back, a small gasp sounding when I finally pull away from her. I keep my face close to hers when I speak, wanting to be sure that she not only hears what I'm saying, but understands it as well. "It is what it is."

Before she can respond, Henry's voice fills the vehicle. "We've arrived Mr. Chase."

Chapter Seven

Holy shit. This guy is saying all the right things. Doing all the right things. It's nice, don't get me wrong. But what am I doing? He's a professional football player. Who lives in a different city than I do. And probably has a girl like me in each city he travels to. I can't let myself get sucked into feeling anything for him, but I'm not sure if I can resist it either. New York and Massachusetts aren't really that far apart from each other after all. I suppose it's possible this could turn into something more. I shake my head to dismiss my own thoughts, turning my attention to the door that's just swung open beside me.

I take the hand he's extending, and step out of the town car onto a sidewalk. His hand immediately slides around my waist, gathering me close, erasing any thoughts I have about where this is going. All I want is to enjoy the here and now, which includes how amazing it feels when he holds me possessively like this; like he's protecting me from the world.

I'm startled a second later when flashbulbs explode to the left of us, Jasper's arm tightening as he hauls me even closer as he mumbles so only I can hear. "Sorry."

"Jasper, who's your date?"

"What happened to Poppy?"

"Mr. Chase, do you think the Patriots will play another super bowl?"

Questions are fired at him as he uses his body to shield me, guiding us into the safety and quiet of the restaurant where a hostess is standing in wait. "I'm so sorry, Mr. Chase." She sweeps an arm out, ushering us further into the entry way of the restaurant. Jasper's arm stays locked around me, but relaxes now that we're inside. "We try to keep the press at a distance, but unfortunately, they sit in wait like vultures for anyone that might show up for dinner with us."

"It's fine." He glances in my direction, his mouth in a tight line, looking at me as if he wants some kind of confirmation. I nod, spots still hindering my vision as I try and blink them away.

"We have a private table ready for you." The hostess starts to walk, still speaking. "We put you upstairs where it will be much quieter."

"You okay?" Jasper tilts his head closer to mine as we follow where we're led. "I should have warned you. It happens sometimes at places like this."

I nod again, still tongue-tied as my brain digests what just happened, specifically the part about Poppy. *Who the hell is Poppy?* I want to ask him, but figure I really don't have any right to at this point in our, whatever you want to label this as, relationship? We're climbing up a set of stairs now, so I focus on those instead, not wanting to trip in my heels. I stay silent as we make our way down a long hall, finally turning into a small room. There are only four tables in the quaint space, but only one of them is set, which has me heaving a sigh of relief I wasn't even aware I was holding.

"You'll have all the privacy you need in here, Mr. Chase." The hostess finally stops moving, a wave of her arm sweeping in an arc across the room. "We'll not seat anyone else in here." She points to the table that's been set. "Please, get comfortable." She turns to leave, still talking. "Roger, your server, will be with you in just a moment."

He guides me to the finely set table, the warmth of his body moving away from me as he releases his hold to pull out a chair for me. I lower myself as gracefully as I can, crossing my ankles under the table when he scoots the chair under my bottom. He takes the seat next to me, rather than the one across from me, his hand covering mine as he sits. "Are you sure you're okay?"

My eyes drift up to his, the corners crinkled as he assesses me with concern. "I promise, I'm fine." I smile, trying to reassure him with more than just words. "Is it like that a lot?"

"It depends." He shrugs. "Sometimes we let the press know when I'm going to be somewhere because we're looking for the publicity. And in those instances, I don't mind cause I'm expecting it." He frowns, his fingers sliding through mine to grip them more tightly. "But when it's in situations like this, it sucks. Not going to lie."

"It wasn't that bad." I say, trying to lighten the mood. "I was only blind for about thirty seconds after we got here."

"Now you know why we always wear sunglasses." He lets out a short laugh. "It's not because we're trying to look cool."

"Who's Poppy?" I blurt out, my curiosity getting the better of me, even though I know I might not like the answer. I feel my cheeks heat as I shift in my chair, sliding my hand out from his to fold it in my lap. I lift my eyes up to his, the soft buttery color seeming to darken as I wait for his reply.

"Poppy McAdams." He's quiet for a second, then continues when he realizes hearing her name means nothing to me. "She's someone I dated."

"But not anymore?"

"No, not anymore." He leans toward me, clearing his throat like he's about to say more, but then sits back suddenly, his focus shifting over my shoulder.

"Good evening, sir." A sharp dressed waiter appears on my left, inclining his head in my direction. "Miss."

"Hello." Jasper and I respond in unison. I think we're both happy with the interruption.

"I'm Roger, and will be at your service this evening." He lays two hand written menus on our place settings, then speaks again. "Would you like a wine menu, or perhaps a cocktail instead?"

Jasper turns his attention to me, a wide smile breaking across his face. "A bottle of Veuve?"

I can't help the tilt of my lips as I try, unsuccessfully, to hide my smile. "Maybe just a glass tonight."

There's a spark in his eye, as his smile grows almost devilish before he addresses the waiter. "We'll have a bottle of Veuve Cliquot if you have it?"

"We do sir." Roger nods. "Two glasses, or something else for you?"

"Just one." He continues. "I'll have an ice water with lemon please."

"Sparkling or still?"

Jesus, its water. Can we move on here? I want to hear more about Poppy, damn it. I tap my foot under the table, my nervous energy needing an escape. I stop when I notice Jasper steal a look in the direction of the noise I'm making.

"Still is fine." The warmth of Jasper's hand covers my leg just above my knee as he responds to Roger. His thumb starts to stroke the inside of my thigh in a slow sweeping motion, melting away the tension I was feeling only a second ago. He fingers splay around my thigh, squeezing gently, as he turns back to me. "Do you trust me?"

I lock my gaze with his and answer without hesitation. "Yes." This is what a single touch from him does to me, and I know in this moment that I'm so screwed. I'm actually falling for this guy. This guy I met less than thirty-six hours ago. He stares back at me, his hold on me relaxing again as his thumb resumes its torturous slide back and forth against my skin when he finally looks back at Roger.

"We'll start with the tomato capri salad, and then we'll both have the boneless rib eye. I'll take mine rare, and the lady will take hers," He turns to look at me so I can fill in the blank.

"Medium" I state, a bit flustered at how turned on I am over his total control of the situation.

He doesn't miss a beat, continuing as soon as I respond. "We'll do the mashed potatoes, grilled asparagus, and the creamed spinach." He turns to me, his brow raised. "Anything else you'd like?"

"Bearnaise sauce?" I suggest, his head whipping back to Roger.

"And bearnaise sauce." He completes our order.

"Very good." Roger nods, clapping his little black folder shut. "I'll get your drinks and be back."

Before Roger is even three feet away, I pounce. "So, you were explaining about Poppy?"

His thumb on my knee stills as a long breath blows from between lips parted in a frown. "As I said, we dated, and now we're not."

"Does she know that?" I can't seem to rein in my jealousy, even though I have absolutely no right to question him. I was the one, just twenty minutes ago in the car, telling him that there were no expectations.

"She knows." His hand leaves my leg and comes to rest on the table in a loose fist. He flexes it a moment before finally speaking. "She's what we refer to in the business as a fame whore. I thought she liked me for me, but came to realize she just liked the attention I brought her." He looks up to look me in the eye. "She means nothing to me."

"It feels like maybe she did?" I continue to question

softly. Not because I'm feeling threatened anymore, but now out of concern for him.

"It's not an easy business to be in if you want to meet someone." He unclenches his fist, moving his hand to lay over mine. "I promise you, I'm fine."

"Okay." I nod, accepting his explanation, and because I want to move on from this topic. "I'm sorry if I pushed."

"You don't have to apologize." He squeezes my hand. "You were just bombarded with flashbulbs and questions. It's okay to ask me what you need to know. I'd rather have you ask me and get the straight answer, instead of googling it to get the twisted truth the media prints."

It seems to be perfect timing on Roger's part again as he enters the room, bottle of champagne in hand, another server shadowing behind him carrying a crystal bucket filled with ice in one hand and a tray with one glass of iced water in the other. They make a bigger production out of opening the bottle then is required in my opinion, but it's a nice way for us to end the topic of Poppy.

When I finally have a glass of champagne in hand, I raise it to Jasper in a toast. "To chance encounters."

I'm rewarded with a wide grin as he lifts his glass to clink against mine lightly. "The very best kind."

That seems to set a new stage for the rest of our evening, which unfolds like a scene from a romance movie, not my life. We talk for two hours straight, while we devour a dinner that may have tasted better than anything I've ever eaten before in my life. For dessert, we share a chocolate soufflé, and finally finish the meal with coffees. We both agree we need the caffeine to keep us from falling into a food coma. I'm full and content, and feel like I've known him for months, not just the one full day it's really been. I've read and of course seen in movies how people will describe how when you meet 'the one' you'll know because the connection is so easy and natural and unlike anything else you've yet to experience. I stare at him, dumbfounded, as we wait in the rear entrance of the restaurant for the car to come around. It occurs to me that I have already fallen for this guy. In one damn day. Holy shit. I'm so totally screwed.

Chapter Eight

She shivers under my arm, and I look down, belatedly realizing she must be cold. How can she not be? She's wearing a sleeveless dress in temperatures that have dropped down to the low sixties. I step away, releasing her so that I can shrug my jacket off. "Here, put this on." Her brows are furrowed, her bottom lip caught between her teeth as she stares at me blankly. "You've got to be freezing." I continue, confused by her expression.

"Oh!" She blurts, the trance she's in breaking as she slides her arms into my jacket, hugging it around her body. "Yes, thank you." She bends her head down to the material of the jacket then lifts it, a smile lighting up her face. "It smells like you."

I chuckle. "That's a good thing?"

She bobs her head once, her smile growing wider. "A very good thing." Her smile is infectious, my lips curving up to mirror hers, a wave of pure adoration crashing over me like the tide, pulling me further into the ocean of feelings I'm treading in. She gets pleasure from the simplest of things, like just the scent of my coat, so very different from what I experienced with other women in my past.

"You're amazing." I cup her face in my hands, unable to resist a second longer. I graze my lips over hers, nipping at them teasingly, savoring the taste of her before I cover her mouth entirely. Her hands snake around my neck, her fingers curling around my nape to pull me closer, our bodies melting together as our kiss deepens. I hear the car approach and reluctantly ease away from her.

Her eyes, hooded and dark, find mine. "What are you doing to me?" She murmurs against my mouth as she leans in to steal one more kiss before stepping away to walk to the car.

I stand for less than a second before snapping to attention. I take wide steps so I can reach the car before her, pulling the door open, my eyes trailing up the length of her bare legs as she curls them under her after sitting. In less than six seconds I'm sitting beside her on the other side of the car, sliding an arm around her waist to yank her up against me. "You're too far away." I explain, in case it isn't obvious.

"I wasn't complaining." Her hand drops on my thigh, just inches from my cock, the close proximity causing it to stir in reaction. I shift, trying to adjust my hips so that her hand will slide a little further down my leg, but instead, she drags it higher. She stops when she bumps against my growing bulge. She turns her body into mine, her other hand planting on my chest as one bare knee slides partially over my leg. My eyes dart to the front of the vehicle when her fingers start to inch their way over my cock, growing harder under her touch.

"What are you doing?" I whisper on a groan as her grip tightens. "Not that I'm complaining."

"It was so cold out there." She practically purrs as her fingers rub the length of my cock, splaying wide as she applies pressure. "Do you mind if I snuggle up to you?" Her voice is flirty and full of innuendo.

"You're playing with fire." I hiss under my breath, using my free hand to clamp over the one she has on my dick, locking it in place. "What about the driver?"

"He thinks we're cuddling after a romantic dinner." One side of her mouth quirks up in a devilish smirk. "Or he thinks I'm back here giving you a hand job." Her fingers clench under my grip, my cock jerking at the attention. "Either way, I'm probably never going to see him again, so I really don't care." She tilts her mouth toward mine, her knee climbing even further up my leg. "So, just kiss me already."

Who am I to argue with that logic? I surge forward, crushing my mouth to hers, transferring my hand to her bare knee. She sweeps her tongue against my lips, urging them open to tangle with my tongue, her hand resuming its torturous grind up and down my cock. It takes every ounce of will power I have not to buck my hips up into her greedy palm, my length throbbing under her touch. Instead, and because it's only fair, I trace my fingers up her smooth skin until I feel the hem of her skirt. I slip my hand underneath, spreading it wide as I slide all the way up to her hip. I continue over the curve of her ass, growling into her mouth when all I find is a thin strip of material in the crack of her ass. She's not commando tonight, but she may as well be.

She whimpers into my mouth when I palm her ass to shove her pussy against my thigh, her hand lifting off my cock to rest beside the other on my chest. Her lips form a silent O when I push against her ass again, my fingers sliding down in between the seam. Heat and moisture seep through the material of my slacks as I hold her tightly against the muscle of my thigh and begin to bounce my leg under her. Her fingers clutch into tiny fists as she grips onto my sweater, her breath panting into my neck now. I tilt my head to whisper in her ear. "Are you warm yet my little spitfire?"

"I'm going to come if you don't stop." She warns, her words hot on my skin as she murmurs against it.

I still my leg, loosening my hold on her at the same time, sliding my hand out from under her skirt. "I'm only stopping because we're back." I crook a finger under her chin to lift her face to mine. "But believe me when I tell you we're not done." I slam my mouth over hers in a searing kiss, sealing the promise of what's to come, pulling back after just a few seconds. "Not even close."

"What are we waiting for?" She pushes off of me to sit up straight, pulling the hem of her skirt back into place. "Let's go." She reaches for the handle just as the door opens from the other side, a hotel valet holding it open. She steps from the car, turning to wait while I slide out behind her. I thank Henry, slip him a hundred for his discretion, then grab Megan's hand as we walk into the hotel. I say a silent thank you when no one from the team is in the lobby, and stride purposely to the elevator, wanting to get to her room as quickly as possible.

"What about your curfew?" She asks as we wait. "Will you get in trouble if you break it two nights in a row?"

"First of all, no one knows I broke anything last night. Doug covered for me, so it's all good." The elevator arrives and we step inside, pressing the button for her floor. "And tonight, the coach thinks I'm staying with my family. They only live a short distance from here."

"Oh." She nods, turning her body to face me, her eyes sweeping up to mine. "So, does that mean you can stay all night?"

I slide my hands around her waist, then move lower to cup her ass, yanking her against me, as I nod. "All night."

"What about practice?" Her hands press flat against my chest as she angles her head to look up at me.

"We have press all morning. No practice tomorrow. I don't have to be there until nine." I stare down into her eyes trying to figure out what's going on in that head of hers, her sudden silence throwing a red flag. "Unless you don't want me to stay." The elevator dings at the arrival of her floor, and the doors slide open. I raise my brows, waiting for a response.

"Come on." She pushes away from my body, but grabs my hand possessively as she leaves the elevator and starts down the hallway. She stops in front of the door to her room, releasing my hand to retrieve the room key out of her purse. Before she can swipe it, I stop her, turning her attention back to me.

"What is it?" I'm confused because five minutes ago she was about to come on my damn leg. Now she seems like she's not sure if she wants this.

"It's nothing." She shakes her head, offering me a small smile. "I was just wondering about tomorrow."

"What about it?" I watch as she brings a finger to her mouth and starts chewing on the nail. I reach for her hand, pulling it away from her teeth. "Talk to me."

"I'm leaving tomorrow." She shrugs. "I'm on a red-eye back to New York. I just-" She shrugs again. "I just hadn't thought about what happens after tonight. Except, now you'll be with me tomorrow. At least in the morning. So, now I'm wondering."

Relief floods through me as I realize it's not about her wanting me to stay versus her possibly just wanting more. "Let's worry about tomorrow, tomorrow." I lean forward to peck my lips against hers. "I promise I won't disappear on you tonight."

"Okay." She breathes out, I think in relief. "Sorry." She swipes the key over the sensor, pushing the door open. "I didn't mean to ruin the moment."

I push the door closed behind me, throwing the deadbolt, then grab her hand to turn her around. "You didn't ruin anything." I move my hands to the lapels of the jacket, pushing it back off her shoulders to slide it off. I step around her, moving further into the room, then drape it over the back of the chair in front of the desk. I smile when I notice the roses placed in the center of the desk. When I turn around, she's already sitting on the bed, her legs crossed as she leans back on her elbows, her gaze roaming down the length of my body.

"Take your sweater off." My brows arch in surprise, but I comply, grabbing the hem with both hands to lift it over my head, tossing it on top of my jacket. "The t-shirt too." She orders, making no excuses for what she wants. I peel that off next, adding it to the growing pile on the chair.

Her tongue darts out to sweep across her lips, my dick twitching, her legs uncrossing as she moves to sit up straight. She blinks, shaking her head. "You're like a damn Greek god."

"Hours of practice and workouts." I explain, taking a step closer. Her hand reaches up to brush down my torso, her fingers skimming lightly over each of the bumps defining my abdomen, stopping when she reaches the belt at my waist. When she lifts her other hand to begin working the buckle, my cock jerks to life, it's length growing hard in seconds. There's no doubt that she notices, one hand straying from the belt when it's undone to stroke it's length, her eyes lifting to lock with mine.

"I've wanted to taste you since last night." The pressure of her hand on my cock increasing slightly as she continues to stroke it through my slacks. "Any objections?"

Her gaze moves slowly down the bare skin of my chest as her fingers begin to release the clasp on my pants. *Is she fucking kidding me right now? Who in their right mind would object?*

She drags the zipper down in one slow pull, my dick jutting out, straining against my boxer briefs as it begs to be set entirely free. She looks up at me, one side of her mouth crooking up. "I'll take that as a no."

She's about to slide her hands inside the waist of my pants, but before she can, I grab her under each arm and yank her up against my body. A gasp of surprise falls from her lips before I slam my mouth over hers, my hands moving to cradle her head as I push my tongue inside to deepen the kiss. Her fingers weave into the longer strands on the top of my head, a moan vibrating between us when I rock my hips into her. After what feels like only seconds, but I know is longer, I tear my lips from hers, short breaths panting from them as I grin. "Definitely no objections."

Her only reply is the slight lift of one eyebrow as her tongue darts out to swipe across my lower lip, her head dipping below my beard a second later. She presses a hot, open mouth kiss to my neck, trailing more of the same down my torso, stopping only to flick her tongue against my belly button. Her ass is on the bed again, but her legs are spread so that they are on either side of mine, her mouth at the waist of my boxers as I tangle my fingers in her hair. She uses her hands to push my pants and boxers down my hips in one hard tug, my cock landing in her mouth as it springs free.

Her mouth is pure, sweet fucking heat around my cock as she inhales me, her hands moving to wrap around the bottom of my shaft. My hips thrust forward on instinct, my hands gripping her scalp to hold her on my cock, her throat closing around it on a gag. *Fuuuccckkk. Why does the sound of her choking on my dick sound so damn good?* I pull my hips back, making sure she can breathe, but her fingers tighten around the base of my cock, her head bobbing forward as she sucks me deeper instead.

A groan rolls out of me from deep in my chest as my head falls back on my shoulders, any coherent thoughts I have evaporating as I let myself just feel. She draws me down into the back of her throat again, swallowing me, than gagging, the action squeezing my cock. She pulls back, and I look down, her spit and my pre-cum dripping from her mouth. She pants heavily before wrapping her lips over me again, sliding all the way down my length, swallowing me. I thrust into her mouth, her lips red and swollen around my cock as she chokes, her eyes popping wide when I buck deeper, keeping her locked in place. "I'm going to come." I chant, pumping my hips again, her fingers digging into the back of my ass as she hums her approval, sucking my cock deep one last time on a swallow as I explode. I cry out as my cum starts shooting down her throat, my knees almost giving out when she continues sucking, swallowing every drop that continues to burst from me until I'm done. My dick pulses one final time as she slides it out of her mouth, her tongue swirling around my softening tip as she slides back on the bed, my hand falling free from her hair.

She's wearing a smile that looks like the cat who ate the canary, her cheeks flushed a dark pink, her lips swollen and wet as she peers up at me under her lashes. I kick my legs free of my trousers, then drop to my knees in front of her, yanking her to my mouth in a feral kiss, as I lean back on my calves. She just delivered the best fucking blow job I've ever had in my life, and I want to return the favor, but my legs are still shaking. I pull away after a moment, resting her forehead on top of mine so I can look her in the eye. "That was fucking incredible."

Her cheeks lift as she smiles, still flushed. "It was my pleasure." She tilts forward pressing her lips to mine for a second. "See for yourself." My brow furrows curiously until she takes one of my hands and slides it under her skirt until it lands between her legs. She's soaked. And swollen. Her pussy throbbing under my hand when I cup it on a growl.

My dick twitches, but it's not quite ready for round two yet, stuck at half-mast for now. But there is no way I'm making her wait for that. I capture her mouth in mine as I push up straight on my knees until I'm almost even with her, then slide a hand around the back of her neck to lower the zipper on her dress. When she feels the slide of my fingers down her bare back, she breaks away from me long enough to allow me to drag the top down around her waist. She's wearing a black lace bra with thin straps that criss-cross across her chest before wrapping around the back of her neck. I'm not sure how it releases, but honestly, I'm not sure if I want to. I skim my fingers over the straps, following them down to the lace material of the bra, before cupping a breast in each hand.

"Do you want me to take it off?" She mewls as I pinch each nipple between my fingers, her back arching into my hands.

I shake my head, my fingers continuing to work her breasts as I push her back onto the bed. "No. It's fucking sexy as hell." I lower myself over one hard peak, and through the lace, I flick my tongue against it. I seal my lips over the fabric and suck, her hips bucking up against mine as she moans, her legs spreading wider as I settle between them. "I like seeing you all strapped up like this." Her fingers glide through the messy strands of my hair as I continue to flick then suck her nipple, her nails digging into my scalp when I grip the hard tip between my teeth and bite softly. She cries out my name, her hips squirming under me, begging for relief. "Jasper, please."

She doesn't have to ask me twice. I slide down the length of her body until I'm bent between her spread legs. The skirt of her dress, although twisted and turned, still covers her center, so I glide my hands up her thighs, moving the material up and over her waist until she's exposed. I draw in a quick breath when my eyes take in her pussy, glistening with wetness around the scrap of lace she thinks serves a purpose. They don't, and I make sure she knows it when I grip the flimsy string with two hands and tear if off her with one tug, a gasp leaving her as her hips jerk from the pressure. "Sorry, they were in the way."

"I don't care." She mewls above me, my fingers stroking at her seam. "You can buy me a new pair." I chuckle, because she's right, I will buy her more. I'll do whatever the hell she wants if this is what I get in return. She's so fucking wet as I press two fingers inside of her, my mouth dropping against her at the same time to run my tongue over her clit. She groans out her approval, her hips jerking up as the walls of her pussy convulse around my fingers. She's so wound up and right on the edge, but I don't want her to come yet, so I lower my tongue, lapping against her folds as I pump my fingers in and out of her. Her arousal is dripping around my fingers, running down into the seam of her ass, coating my beard with each graze of my tongue.

I keep lapping her folds, but can't resist sliding out of her to run my fingers over the hole of her ass, curious if she'll like it. My dick juts fully to life when instead of pushing away, she bears down on my fingers, purring her approval from above. "Yes, just like that." She lets out a guttural moan when I press a finger against her opening and push in to the first knuckle, my mouth moving to suck her clit back into my mouth at the same time. "God, yes! Yes!" She urges me on, shoving her ass down onto my hand until my finger is all the way inside of her, my dick throbbing against my stomach in approval. I slide my finger out, then place a second finger at her hole, easing them both all the way in. Her head begins to thrash back and forth as she pants out her approval when I start to pump them slowly in and out of her. I flick her clit, then bite down, sucking hard as I slam my fingers against her ass, a scream erupting from her as she starts to come. Every muscle below her waist tightens for several long seconds, then begins to pulsate around my fingers and under my mouth, her legs relaxing around my head.

I pump in and out of her a few more times, my tongue laving over her folds, the taste of her even sweeter now that she's come. My cock is throbbing below my waist, her wet center a siren call. I slide my fingers out of her, rising myself up and over her body, propping myself beside her. She turns her face to mine, a content smile dancing across her lips. "Hi."

"Hi yourself." I drawl out. "I want to kiss you so bad

right now, but there's so much of you in my beard, it might be a little gross."

"I don't care." She reaches out, gripping my beard in her fingers to pull my face to hers and kisses me. I open wide, thrusting my tongue into her mouth, loving that she has no inhibitions at all about the taste of herself. I shift my weight, rolling my body over hers, my cock, hard and heavy pressing into her dress, wedged between us, as I feast on her, her flavor intoxicating.

She wrenches her mouth off mine. "You're hard again." Her hand snakes between our bodies to curl around my shaft, my eyes closing with her grip as I nod.

Her legs spread underneath mine, my eyes flying open when I feel her line my cock up to her core. "You want more?"

"God, yes." She shifts her pelvis under me. "I thought we determined last night that once wasn't enough."

I half groan, half laugh, not quite believing this girl can be this entirely perfect. Without further discussion, I give her what she wants, driving my hips forward, burying myself inside her heat in one thrust. She's so fucking wet as I drag my cock in and out of her, slowly at first, my thrusts increasing, becoming harder with each stroke.

"Yes." Her fingers cling to my back, her nails breaking the skin each time I piston into her, sweat breaking across my body in a thin sheen. "Harder." She drives her hips up into mine, meeting me thrust for thrust. "God, you fuck so good." As if it was even possible, my dick grows harder, her words, her need, inflaming my desire, taking me to new heights.

"You want more baby?" I pant, pumping my dick into her, my balls finally beginning to tighten as my release starts to build.

"Yes." She chants each time I drive into her, me on my knees now, my hands gripping her hips as I drive into her again and again. "God, don't stop Jasper. Don't stop!" Her walls suddenly grip my cock in a tight, vise-like hold, her mouth dropping open as she lets out a moan. I jerk my hips back and then slam into her, my length sinking deep in her pussy as I roar out my release, our bodies throbbing together as we come, the heat of my cum drowning my cock as I collapse on top of her.

Chapter Nine

"Jasper, you're crushing me." I grunt out, gripping his biceps as I try and push him off me. *Sweet Jesus he weighs a lot!*

"Sorry." He mumbles next to my ear, his arms flexing under my hold as he pushes off my body, then shifts back to rest on his knees between my legs. He scrubs a hand down his beard, a smirk lifting one side of his mouth. "Lost my head there for a minute."

I nod, staying silent as I shamelessly ogle his body again. Greek. Fucking. God. And didn't the Greek gods normally have beards in all the photos I've seen? I'm going to have to look that up. "What nationality are you?" My ability to keep my thoughts and curiosity contained, always a problem.

"That's random." He chuckles, scooting back off the bed to stand. "American?" He shrugs, turning to walk into the bathroom. I sit up on the bed, but my dress, still tangled around my waist, makes it difficult to actually bend, so I slide to the edge and stand. He appears in front of me a second later with a wash cloth. "I didn't know if you needed this?"

"Oh." I take it from him, surprised at this thoughtfulness. "Thank you." I point to the bathroom. "I'm just going to go take my dress off." I step around him to head to the bathroom. "Be right back."

"Okay." He turns, watching me as I scoot into the room and shut the door behind me. I take a look at myself in the mirror and cringe in horror. The back of my hair looks like, well, hell's bells, like I just got laid, and half my mascara is under my eyes. I let out a silent groan, tossing the wash cloth onto the counter so I can use both hands to push my dress down over my waist, stepping out of it when it hits the floor. I pick it up, shake it out, then lay it on the back of the toilet. Next, I work the clasp behind my neck to release my bra, throwing it on top of the dress.

I glance at the shower, the urge to rinse off strong, but wage an internal war with myself about the rudeness of leaving Jasper alone in the room that long. Instead I use the toilet, then the wash cloth to clean up below my waist. I splash some water on my face, making sure to wipe the mascara off completely, and last but not least, run a brush through my hair. My robe is hanging on the back of the door, so I wrap it around my body, securing it loosely with the tie. I take one last look in the mirror, then open the door, freezing when I step out of the bathroom.

He's sound asleep. The covers are pulled up to his waist, his bare chest rising and falling gently, a soft snore sounding each time he exhales. He's lying on his back, one arm flung over his head on the pillow, while the other one lies relaxed next to his side. He must have been exhausted from being up late last night, then practice today, and now another late night with me. I walk over to the desk to snap the lamp off, pausing when I notice his t-shirt. I skim my fingers over the soft cotton, then gather the material, lifting it off the chair. I raise it to my nose and inhale deeply, closing my eyes when his scent invades my nostrils. I decide then and there that I'm wearing it to bed. I drop the shirt back onto the chair long enough to strip my robe off, then grab it again to pull over my head. The hem swishes against the middle of my thighs as the material settles around me, enveloping me in all things Jasper. I smile at the simple pleasure his t-shirt brings me. I snap off the light, then tip-toe to the bed, sliding in beside him.

I blink awake, then close my eyes, my mind working to piece together what woke me. I hear the toilet flush, then remember I'm not alone. Jasper's here with me. I slide my eyes open again when the bathroom door opens, the room remaining dark as he treads softly across the carpet toward the bed. It dips as he sits, then again when lays back, his legs slipping gingerly under the covers.

"Hey." I say in a hushed tone, rolling onto my side to face him.

"Hey." He turns so that he's facing me. "I'm sorry. I didn't mean to wake you up."

"It's okay. " I can see the outline of his face and the

shadow of his beard through a crack of light coming in through the closed curtains. "What time is it?"

"A little after two." His fingers are suddenly in my view, and then gone as he brushes them down through my locks. "I actually wondered if you slept with your hair up or down."

I can't help the smile that appears at the result of his confession. "Actually, I usually sleep with it up. Just piled into a messy bun on top of my head. I roll around a lot when I sleep and it gets stuck under me if I don't. I wake myself up pulling my own hair." I giggle softly. "How's that for sexy?"

"Well, I think you're beautiful, no matter how you wear your hair." He murmurs, his fingers leaving my hair to float over my cheek, his head tilting to mine as he sweeps a kiss against my lips.

I don't think I'm a vain person. I usually don't even spare myself a second glance in a mirror once I've gotten ready for the day. But, I know I'm pretty. I've been told by enough people to believe it, and the attention I get from men reiterates it. But when *he* tells me I'm beautiful, it's the first time I've actually ever felt it. Even as I lay here with my hair in tangles, my face free of make-up, and wearing just his t-shirt. He makes me feel like the most beautiful girl on the planet. "Thank you." I whisper, my words catching in my throat as I also realize that the more time I spend with Jasper, the harder I'm falling for him.

"I'm a mutt by the way." His head is back on his pillow now, but he's still connected to me, his fingers a breezy touch on my arm as he strokes them up and down my skin.

"What?" I'm confused for a second, then remember I had asked him earlier what his nationality was. I let out a small laugh. "I guess most American's probably are."

"Yeah, I mean I know I've got some Greek, Scottish and German in me." He stops talking when I let out a guff of laughter, his forehead crinkling. "What's so funny?"

"Sorry." I suck my lips into a straight line between my teeth, trying to quell my outburst, popping them out so I can explain. "Every time I see you with your shirt off, all I can think is, Greek god." I lift my shoulders in a shrug. "At least I know I wasn't far off."

He laughs. "What about you?" He stills his fingers, then moves his hands under his pillow to prop his head up a little higher. "What's your heritage?"

"Swedish mostly. On my mom's side." I shift up a little on my own pillow so I'm level with him. "And Welsh I guess. My dad's grandparents moved here from Wales when they were in their twenties. I think right before World War II started."

"Are they still alive?" He pauses, then continues, clarifying his question. "Your great grandparents? Can you imagine the things they've seen change in this world?"

"My great grandmother is. But my not my great granddad." I let out a small sigh as I remember him and the way he always called me Meg Pie in his clipped Welsh accent. "He died about five years ago." I'm silent for a minute then speak again. "Actually my middle name is after him. So, I guess I'll always have a piece of him with me."

"What is it?"

"Okay, but don't laugh. It's kind of a strange name for a girl."

"I promise not to laugh at yours if you don't laugh at mine." He challenges, his brow arching high.

"Oh, this is getting interesting." I chuckle. "You have a deal."

"You go first."

"It's Fitzpatrick." I scrunch my nose up as I wait for his reaction.

"Megan Fitzpatrick Lewis." He gives me a warm smile. "I love it. It fits you."

"Okay, tell me yours." I fold my hands under my cheek on my pillow, propping myself a little higher. "I'm dying to know now."

"First, I have to give you the back ground story." He shifts in the bed, adjusting himself so his face is even with mine on his pillow. "When my mom was pregnant, she discovered Jane Austen and started devouring all her books. She became a infatuated with everything she wrote, but especially Pride and Prejudice. She decided she wanted to name me Darcy, after Mr. Darcy." He pauses. "Wait, have you read Pride and Prejudice?"

"Does watching the movie count?" I shrug my shoulders.

"Probably not in my mother's eyes, but as long as you know what I'm talking about." He reaches his hand over to mine and pulls it into his before he continues. "Anyway, my dad wouldn't allow it. He hated the name and said it sounded to girly. So, they made a deal and he got to pick my first name and she could pick my middle name."

"Okay, you're killing me here." I wave my hand in the air

in an attempt to move the story along. "What name did she pick? Are you Jasper Darcy?"

"Bennet." He states, then elaborates. "Jasper Bennet." He looks at me waiting for a response, but when I don't say anything, he heaves out a breath and continues. "You know, after Jane. Jane Bennet."

"Oh!" The light bulb finally goes off in my head. "I get it! That's actually pretty cool!"

"Right?" He breaks into a wide grin. "I bet you don't know anyone else with that name."

"Nope." I chuckle, the delight he takes in his name so endearing.

"I've already decided when I have a son, that's what I'm going to name him. And I can call him Ben or Benny for short."

"That's really sweet, Jasper." I lean forward and brush a soft kiss against his lips.

We spend the next three hours talking. Just lying next to each other, sometimes our hands touching, sometimes stopping to press our lips against each other, but our questions about each other, our lives, our desires, seeming endless. So, when he asks the next question, it jars me for a minute as I realize I'm going to have to say goodbye to him.

"What time does your plane leave tonight?" His voice is hushed, like he really doesn't want to know the answer, but also needs to at the same time.

"Ten-thirty."

"Would you consider staying a few more days?" His hand slides over my check to cup it in a soft hold. "I can pay for a new flight, or the change fee, and for more nights here at the hotel."

My heart stutters in my chest, tripping over each syllable falling from his lips, leaving me momentarily speechless. Perhaps taking my silence as doubt, he starts rambling with reasons to stay. "I can be free after two so we can spend this afternoon together. My parents arrive tomorrow, so they'll take up some of my time, unless you want to meet them of course, then you could just be with me. And I can get you a ticket to the game on Sunday as well. I'd love to have you see me play."

"Jasper." I squeeze my fingers around his to get his attention, his mouth closing as his eyes dart to mine. "I'll stay."

"You will?" He laughs, his cheeks lifting as he breaks into a wide smile. "Really?"

"Really."

Before I can say anything more, he surges forward, crushing his mouth to mine, his lips still curved up. After a moment he pulls back, still smiling, his other hand shifting to cup my cheek. "Are you sure?"

"Are you?" I chuckle, wanting to make sure he knows what he's actually asking.

"Yes." He presses another kiss to my lips. "I want more time with you."

"What about practices though, and your family? And don't you have press stuff tomorrow? I don't want--" I'm about to say more but he silences me by covering my mouth with his. He lingers there long enough to momentarily quiet my concerns, my mind blank when he pulls away.

"We only have one light practice tomorrow. My parents aren't arriving until tomorrow afternoon. Press is this morning, and then I'm free." He smooths a hand over my cheek. "I can make time for you. I want to."

I nod under his touch. "Okay." I turn my head into his palm and press a kiss against it. "I don't need you to pay for my flight and room though."

"But, I want to." His hand moves to stroke through my hair. "It's the least I can do."

I shake my head. "I'd rather you didn't." I offer him a small smile. "But it means more than you know that you're offering."

"Well, you're going to have to take the ticket for the game from me, cause it's sold out, and it's the only way you're getting in." He chuckles, apparently the satisfaction of this one win giving him a reason to celebrate.

"Fine." I state, trying to sound defeated. "I'll have no idea what's going on the entire game, but I promise you I'll be screaming your name the loudest from the stands."

"Kinda like earlier?" His brows arch as his mouth quirks up in a coy smile, moving over me before I can react. His body is propped over mine, his strong arms flexed beside my head, his beautiful toffee colored eyes staring down into my blue ones as he waits for my answer.

I grin, my hands coming to rest on his bushy beard so I can cradle his face. "Yes, kinda like that, but even louder."

"It gets louder?" He jokes, bending to drop a kiss to my lips, speaking against them as he does. "Wanna prove it?"

I giggle, my lips vibrating against his before I murmur my reply. "Well, practice does make perfect."

"You're so fucking right." He ends any further discussion between us for the next twenty minutes, and I'm sure, even though they may not have been as loud as they would be in a stadium, my screams at least woke the person on the other side of the wall from us.

Chapter Ten

"You must really like this chick if you're bailing on us again." I snap my gaze to Doug. We just finished four hours of press rounds, and I'm back in the room so I can change out of my suit into more casual clothes.

"How the hell am I bailing on you?" I counter, unable to reel in the anger lacing my tone. "You need me to hold your fucking hand while you jerk off?" I wrestle my jacket onto a hanger then slam it on the rack in the closet. "Seriously, man. What's your problem?"

"You should be spending more time with the team." I stop what I'm doing to look at Doug. He's leaning against the desk, his arms folded across his wide chest, his face red with anger. "Your head isn't going to be in the game on Sunday and we need your fucking head in the game. You're our most valuable receiver."

"My head will be in the game." I unbuckle the belt at my waist and rip it out of the loops in one yank. "I've played in three fucking super bowls, and won two of them. I know what's expected of me." I stride over to the dresser and pull a drawer open to grab a pair of jeans. "If you want to worry about something, worry about your own damn self." I slam the drawer then stride into the bathroom.

"I'm just fine." Doug yells from the other side of the door. "Thank you very much!"

I change quickly into the jeans, then storm back into the bedroom. "So am I. So get off my damn ass." I point a finger at him, my voice rising. "I'm at every practice, every event, on the field for every game, and bust my ass every single fucking time. This girl-" I clench my teeth, shaking my head before speaking again. "*No* girl is going to get in the way of how I play when I step on that field on Sunday."

"Why didn't you just say that to begin with?" Doug shrugs, rolling his eyes as his mouth curves into a smile.

"You're a fucking asshole, man." I pick the belt off the bed and snap it at him, relief washing over me when I realize he's over whatever this is.

"You breaking curfew again tonight?" He drawls the question out slowly, his implication obvious.

Okay, maybe he's not as over it as I thought. I blow out a slow breath before I answer, glancing his way when I do. "If the choice is between sleeping in here with your ass or up against hers, which one do you think I'm going to choose?"

"Got it." Doug pushes off the desk, brushing past me as he heads in the direction of the door. "I'm outta here. Gonna go meet up with White to study routes." He tosses me one last look over his shoulder on his way out. "You know where we'll be if you want to join us."

Yeah, he's definitely not okay. That was a not so subtle dig about me not focusing my attention where he thinks I should be. I don't even bother answering. It's not worth it. We both said what we needed to say. And my mind is made up. I'm grabbing Megan from her room later and can't wait to share the surprise I've got planned for us.

At precisely three, I knock on her door, my breath catching in my throat when she pulls the door open. She's stunning, in the most natural way, light freckles scattered over her nose and cheeks, her hair plaited in a long braid over her shoulder. I step into her, sliding one hand around the nape of her neck to draw her mouth to mine. I inhale, her taste already becoming a comfort to me, then kiss her, every muscle in my body relaxing from her touch. I pull away after a moment, my lips unable to do anything but lift into a smile when I'm with her. "Hey."

"Hey." She repeats softly. She steps back out of my hold, pulling the door wider. "Come in."

I walk further into the room, turning around to face her once I'm inside. "You look beautiful."

Her brow furrows as she looks down the length of her body then back at me. "I'm wearing jeans and a sweatshirt."

I cock my head. "It's not about what you're wearing." How can she not know that about herself? That it's about who she is, and how she looks at me. Before she can ask me to explain, I shift the conversation. "Besides, it's perfect for where I want to take you."

"But wait." Her face breaks into an ear-splitting grin as she holds up her index finger. "I have a surprise for you."

I cock my head, curious. "Okay."

She grabs the hem of the sweatshirt and slowly lifts. So far I'm liking this surprise. Is it wrong to hope she's wearing nothing underneath? But after another second, I figure it out, my eyes rolling up to the ceiling when she finally pulls the garment off with an exaggerated flourish. "Ta-Da!"

She's wearing a fitted t-shirt emblazoned with the Patriots logo and my jersey number on it. "Something you just had in the closet?" I scrub my hand over my beard to try and keep my smile hidden. She looks fucking hot in it, I'll give her that.

"I went shopping after I left the hospital today." She smiles proudly, twirling around to show me the back. I chuckle when I read my name across the back, Property of Chase. She spins around to face me, still grinning like a loon. "And I got an official game jersey with your number to wear on Sunday."

"I would have given you one of mine." I say, hating that she spent money on something I could give her for free.

"Now you tell me." She laughs, her hand fisting on her hip as she juts it out. "You must be really popular because there were about ten different shirts with your name on them."

I nod then chuckle under my breath, still a little shocked that she truly has no idea, nor does she seem to care, that I'm a well-known player in the league. "Yeah, I guess so."

"I only have these to wear for shoes though." She kicks one foot out in front of her, covered in a white chuck. "I know you said boots, but it's these or heels."

"They're fine." I hold out the jacket I have in my hand. "You're going to need this too."

She slides it from my grasp, her mouth curving down into a frown as she holds it up. It's a fitted, black leather jacket, with a thin fleece lining. "You bought me a jacket?" She swings her gaze up to mine. "I have my sweatshirt I can wear."

"Borrowed." I take the jacket from her fingers and open it, bobbing my head to indicate she should put it on. "From my sister." She turns and slides her arms into the sleeves. "You look about the same size as her." She spins around adjusting the leather on her shoulders. "And yep, it looks like I was right. It fits perfectly."

"It's nice." She shrugs as she nods. "But I could have worn the one I have with me."

"I wasn't sure what you had, and wanted to make sure you had the right thing to wear." I lean forward and peck a kiss on her cheek. "It looks way better on you than her anyway."

"Okay smooth talker." She gives me an exaggerated eye roll. "What else do I need?"

"Just sunglasses if you have them. If not, I can grab you some while we're out." I purse my lips in thought then shrug. "I think that's it."

"Do you think I'd come to L.A. without a pair of sunglasses?" She grins widely, then turns to the desk to rifle through her computer bag, finally pulling a glass case free. After waving it in the air in triumph, she opens it, grabs the glasses, then slides them over her nose.

I let out a huff of laughter, then pull a pair out of my jacket pocket and slide them on. "We're too fucking cool for school."

She joins my laughter, then comments. "I'm also wholly prepared for any surprise paparazzi that jumps out at us now too."

"There is that." I drag a hand over my beard as I recall the night before. "I'm pretty sure we'll be okay where I'm taking you."

"If you say so." She snags her room key off the desk and slides it into the front pocket of her jeans, then takes her phone and zips it into one of the pockets on the coat. "Let's go then."

We leave the room and grab an elevator. I push the button for one of the garage levels instead of the lobby, her head tilting when she notices, but she stays silent instead of questioning it. When the doors slide open, I lead her around the corner from the elevator, stopping when I notice her feet have frozen in place.

"Nope." Her head is swinging back and forth as her arms cross over her chest. "Not happening."

"Seriously?" I walk over to her, snaking one of her hands out of her hold to drag her closer to the object of her obvious disapproval. "Come on. I promise I'm an excellent driver."

"Do you know how many people die in motorcycle accidents a year? I am not getting on that death trap." She shakes her head firmly, arms crossing again. "How do you even have a motorcycle here anyway?"

"My dad dropped it off earlier for me." My head falls back against my shoulders, a frustrated breath blowing between my lips as I look up at the ceiling. After a second, I lower my gaze to find hers. "Have you ever even ridden on one?"

She diverts her gaze, her foot beginning to tap nervously as she responds, her voice hesitant. "No."

Hope blooms as I realize fear is driving her to say no, and not the fact that she doesn't actually enjoy riding on a motorcycle. She's never even been on one before. "Listen, Megan, I promise I'll take extremely good care of you, and will follow every speed limit and street sign. I think you'll really like it if you give it a chance."

Her foot stops tapping and she turns to face me. "I'm scared." Her eyes go wide as she continues. "What if I fall off the back, or lean too far when you go around a corner and I make the bike tip over? Or what if someone doesn't see us and hits us? You have a really big game on Sunday."

I chuckle as I move closer to gather her in my arms. "First of all, you're not going to fall off the back. You're going to wrap your arms around me and not let go. You just push your body up to mine and if I lean, you lean with me." She's looking down at my chest, and not up at me, so I place a finger under her chin to lift her eyes to mine. "And baby, you could get hit walking across the street. You can't not do shit out of fear. I'm a good driver. I make sure to pay extra attention to what other drivers are doing around me when I'm on a bike." I release my hold on her, but grab her hand to drag her closer to the bike, letting go when we reach it. "And look, I even have a helmet for you." I snag it off the handlebar and hold out it to her.

She takes it from my extended hand, then bounces it up and down in her grasp like she's testing its weight. Her lip is turning into mincemeat as she grinds it between her teeth as she seems to wage an internal battle over riding with me. She starts pacing back and forth, and when I can't stand the indecision any longer, I step in front of her. She stops and I slide my hand around her neck to bring her forehead to mine. "I'll take care of you."

"You promise?"

I tilt forward to brush a kiss against her lips. "I promise."

A breath of resignation puffs against my mouth a second before she finally consents. "Okay." She pushes her lips against mine in a quick kiss then steps back, swinging the helmet up and over her head. "Help me buckle this?"

"Sure." I take the straps from under her chin and work to fasten them.

"Stop smiling like that." She mutters.

"Like what?" My cheeks are actually a little sore from how wide I'm grinning.

"Like you just won the lottery." She grumbles. "You're going to be sorry if I fall off that damn bike."

"You better hold on tight then." I peck her lips softly, then step back to put my own helmet on. "Besides, I think you're the one that actually won the lottery."

Her head cocks. "How's that?"

I swing my leg over the bike then lower myself onto the seat. I use one foot to kick the stand up, then balance the bike between my legs as I motion to her. "Climb on." I nod toward the back tire. "Put your foot on that peg and then just hop up onto the seat behind me."

She does as I instruct, her hands gripping onto my

shoulders as she steps onto the peg to clamber over the seat, scooting her body as close to mine as she can when she's behind me.

"See?" I pat her hands, already clutched in a death grip around my waist. "Winner."

"What?" She quips. "How?"

"You get to squeeze me between your thighs for the next hour. On a vibrating seat." I chuckle. "I think you're the clear winner here."

She releases her hold on me to give me a playful slap on the arm. "Jasper!"

"You'll see." I chuckle again. "You ready?"

"I guess so." She breathes against the back of my neck. "Please be careful."

"Always." I press the button to start the bike, her arms clamping around my middle again, then I put it into gear and drive us out of the garage and into the California sunshine.

Chapter Eleven

He was right. The vibration of the seat under me. My legs wrapped tightly around his. My hands keeping me tethered to him. I love it all. But it's also the things he didn't tell me; I'm sure because they are things you can only experience for yourself. The feeling of freedom as we fly down the highway. The way the sun feels against your face. How giving complete control of my life to someone else makes me feel more alive than I ever have before. It's euphoric. I want to throw my head back and scream from the top of my lungs because it feels so amazing. But I don't. Instead, I squeeze him closer, silently thanking him for this experience, reveling in the pure joy it's bringing me.

As we cruise down the Pacific Coast Highway, I totally understand why he wanted to take his motorcycle. The view of the ocean as we drive North is nothing short of stunning. I have no idea what our destination is, but he did say we'd be riding around an hour, so assume we must be getting close. I'm not wrong, and less than ten minutes later, the bike slows as he downshifts, turning into a parking lot. It's situated on a bluff overlooking the blue water, picnic tables scattered along a fence lining the small perimeter.

The engine on the bike quiets as he switches it off, his booted foot kicking the stand down at the same time he pulls his helmet off. He shakes his head, his hair ruffling, and it's then that I realize I'm still holding onto him. I loosen my grip around his waist and slide back a couple inches. I immediately miss the heat of his body, but stare down in amazement at the humming I feel between my legs. Okay, yeah. I'm definitely enjoying these unknown benefits of being a biker chick. He rises, then steps off the bike, his body twisting as he does so that he's facing me when both feet are planted on the ground again.

He sets his helmet on the seat, then looks up at me. He's smiling. It's a smile so broad and so full of obvious joy that I can't help when my cheeks rise in response. He steps closer, and begins working the buckle under my chin. "You liked it."

"I loved it." I confirm, the smile on my face growing wider.

"I knew you would." He stretches the helmet away from my ears, then pulls it off my head. He uses one hand to smooth down locks that must have strayed from my braid, then slides it lower to cup my cheek. He kisses me. His lips warm and soft against my own, the action so tender it leaves me feeling utterly possessed.

When he starts to pull away, I cover his hand with my own to keep him close. "Thank you, Jasper."

He doesn't ask what for. He just nods, accepting my gratitude with another soft kiss before helping me off the back of the bike. It's this moment. This very simple moment, that I know I've fallen in love with him. My vision swirls in a slow haze as I suck in a deep breath, and my hand claws outward for balance until it lands on his forearm.

"Whoa." He drops the helmet, freeing his other hand to grab my shoulder to hold me steady. "What's wrong?"

I blink, trying to clear the fuzz at the edges of my sight, his crinkling eyes the first thing I see as they come into focus a second later. "Nothing." I step into him, wrapping my arms around the security of him, hoping he can't feel how hard my heart is beating. I bury my face in the opening of his jacket, pressing my cheek against the warmth of his chest. "I just got a little dizzy." His arms flex around me when I fuse myself more tightly against him as I try to come up with a plausible explanation. "Maybe a little motion sickness from the bike." I'm afraid if he sees my face right now, he'll know I'm lying, so I stay in the comfort of his arms until he eases me back.

"You okay now?" It's clear from the tone of his voice he's concerned, and I want to nod my head yes, but all I can do is stare up at him as a thousand thoughts scream in my head. *I am in love with him! This doesn't happen after three days. What do I do now? Do I tell him? No, he'll freak out. It's been three damn days! Breathe Megan, just breathe.* He draws me back into his arms when I don't answer, his voice soft against my ear. "Just take a minute to get your feet under you." *I'm so fucked.*

I let him hold me for a minute, willing my heart rate to slow to a somewhat normal rhythm as I blow out a few long breaths, then extract myself from his arms. "I'm okay." I smile, trying to reassure him.

"You sure?"

He keeps one hand anchored to my arm until I nod, forcing out a small laugh to try and hide my mortification.

"Positive." I bend down to retrieve the helmet he dropped a few moments ago, then hold it up in question. "Where should I put this?"

He takes it, then hangs it from one of the handlebars, his eyes sweeping up and down my frame as he assesses me. He finally nods like he's satisfied, then moves to unzip and shrug off the jacket he's wearing. "We can keep our jackets here if you want." I watch as he lifts the seat to reveal a hidden storage space.

I step over and peer inside the secret compartment. "Huh, that's handy." I grin, mostly in relief that he seems to be buying my story, but also because I am actually hot with this jacket on now that we've stopped. I take it off, grab my cell out of the pocket, then fold it before handing it to him. He stuffs it inside my helmet, then crams it down on top of his jacket, snapping the seat back into place.

"Have I mentioned how much I like seeing my number on you?" His fingers trace over the 11 displayed on my chest, a sly grin lifting one corner of his mouth before he drops a kiss to my lips. "Come on." He snatches my hand drawing me beside him as he starts to walk to a set of stairs along the fence. "I want to show you one of my favorite places."

I pause when we reach the top of the stairs, the view before me stealing the breath from me. "Wow." I glance at him, my eyes wide, then shift my attention forward again. "This is so beautiful."

"Yep." He states quietly. I shift my gaze when I realize he's staring at me and not the view. Vertigo tickles at the edges of my brain once more as my eyes lock with his, and I wonder if I'll ever feel like I'm on solid ground again when I'm with him. Before I can say anything, he tugs my hand and starts down the stairs. The beach isn't long, but also not short enough to be considered a cove either. There are tall rock formations spread all along its length and along the cliff wall, some with wide arches you can see through.

I'm not sure if it's because it's January, and to most locals, not prime weather for being at the beach, or because the size of the parking lot is so small, but the place is mostly deserted. I only see a few other people walking or sitting on the sand. It's actually a really warm afternoon, the temperature is in the mid-seventies and the sky a brilliant blue, so I think we must be lucky to have the entire beach almost to ourselves.

We reach the bottom of the stairs and step onto the damp, packed sand, birds scattering in the breeze as we walk closer to the water's edge. I can't stop staring at the rocky columns spread across the beach, each one a unique shape and size. "Those are the coolest things." I point to one a bit farther down the beach from us that has a large open center that you can see the waves through. "I want to take my picture in that one."

"Yeah, this is a really popular place for the locals to come to for their prom and wedding pictures. It can get pretty crowded down here around sunset."

"I can see why." I let go of his hand and break into a run, shouting to him over my shoulder as I sprint in the direction of the large arch. "Come on! I'll race you!"

I'm not sure what I was even thinking challenging a professional athlete to a race, because even though I'm running as hard as I can, he catches me in less than five seconds. I hear his footsteps stomping against the surf before I feel him, his arms scooping me up from behind. He locks me against his chest and then spins us in circles, my laughter loud as my arms clutch around his neck. He stops short and swings his arms out like he's going to toss me in the surf. His amusement carries on the wind when I yelp loudly in protest, my grip tightening as I hold onto him for dear life.

He lowers his mouth to mine, capturing it in a breathy kiss. When he pulls away, a wide smile splays across his face. "God, I love-" He pauses for less than a second, but it's long enough for me to notice, even though he continues like it didn't happen. "-hearing you laugh." He presses another kiss against my lips, then sets me back on my feet. "Let's go take some pictures before the sun sets."

I nod, my voice temporarily stuck in my throat, closing my fingers around his when he takes my hand as we continue our trek to the largest of the arched rock formations. "I had my first real kiss on this beach." He says it quietly, his nose scrunching up a tiny bit as he shakes his head at the memory. "I was fifteen and had come with a group of friends after our Sophomore Social. It was a full moon that night and we thought it would be cool to take some pictures down here while we were all dressed up." We reach the arch and he pulls me into the center of it. "I remember standing right here, feeling like the luckiest bastard in the world as she let me kiss her." He chuckles. "Her name was Melissa. She got married last year to someone she met in college."

He turns, surprising me when he draws me into his arms, leaning over me until his lips are a fraction from mine. He speaks, his breath hot against my own as his words reach my ears. "Little did I know that moment would have nothing on this one." Any coherent thought I have is obliterated the second his lips claim mine in a kiss so searing my knees literally go weak under me. His hold on me tightens as his tongue sweeps against mine, a groan vibrating between us as we melt into one. In this moment, I don't know where I end and where he begins, and I wonder how I'll ever walk away at the end of the weekend.

When he finally pulls away, he drops a single kiss to the tip of my nose then releases me, a small smile tugging at his lips. "You know we're going to have to figure out what happens after this weekend, right?"

Can he read my freaking mind? "New York and Boston really aren't that far away." My fingers find the end of my braid and start fidgeting with it as another question pops into my head. "Wait, do you even live in Boston? Do you guys play all year round?"

He lets out a loud laugh, his head falling back as it rumbles up through his chest. After a second, he looks back down at me. "You're fucking adorable, you know that?"

"Don't mock me." I pout. "I told you I don't follow sports at all."

He leans over and plants a kiss on my forehead, still smiling broadly. "I know, it's what I love about you the most."

I freeze. There's that word again. It doesn't seem to faze him in the slightest this time though, because he continues without stopping. "We only have games in the fall. And we only play in the early winter if we make the playoffs. We technically get the winter and spring off, but honestly, we never stop training."

He takes the braid from my fingers, I think to keep me from destroying the ends of my hair, as he continues. "I have a place in Boston, but I have a place in West Hollywood too. I usually stay here in the off season. Boston's fucking cold in the winter!" He laughs tugging me into his arms again. "But for you I might be able to sacrifice a few cold weekends." He brushes his lips to mine. "We'll figure it out."

"I'll make sure I volunteer for any West Coast implementations this winter." I smile back at him.

"See? We're already figuring things out." He kisses me one more time, then releases me, pulling his phone out of his back pocket. "Ready for your close-up?"

We spend the next half-hour posing for pictures in the arch, near the arch, on the beach, and wrapped in each other's arms. The sun is just starting to set as we climb up the stairs to the parking lot, so when we reach the top, we take a few sunset pictures there as well. It's been a perfect afternoon, and I tell Jasper just that as he's strapping my helmet on. "Thank you for a perfect California afternoon."

He gazes into my eyes for several long seconds before he

responds, his face more serious than I've seen it before. "It's been a good day." Then he kisses me softly. "Ready to go back?"

"Back to the real world?" I sigh, watching as he slides his helmet on.

He flashes a cocky grin. "Well, we might be able to avoid the real world for one more night."

"A perfect ending to our perfect day?" I grin mischievously, more than willing for whatever he has in mind.

He throws his leg over the bike, straddling the seat to kick up the stand before sitting down. He motions for me to climb on behind him. I use the peg to hop on behind him, then glide my hands around his waist, locking them together, holding him tight. This time, I'm not afraid when he zooms out of the parking lot onto the highway. I'm warm and content and have never felt safer in someone's care. Too bad I have absolutely no clue that nothing is ever as perfect as it seems.

Chapter Twelve

I glance at my watch as I step off the bike. It's just after six-thirty. We made good time getting back to the hotel, considering it's a Friday night in Los Angeles and traffic is usually a nightmare. I pull my helmet off, hang it on the handlebar, then turn to help Megan off. "You dizzy this time?"

"Oh." Her brows jump up as she seems to consider my question. "Nope." Her fingers find the strap under her chin as she tries to figure out the buckle. "Guess I got used to the feeling." I chuckle when she lets out a frustrated huff, tossing her hands in the air. "I can't get this stupid thing."

"Let me." I release the strap in less than three seconds, and instead of being met with gratitude, she rolls her eyes.

"Do you have to be good at everything?" She muses as I pull the helmet off her head.

"Well, I don't know if I *have* to be," I flash her my cockiest grin, "but apparently I am." I seal my proclamation with a loud smack of my lips against hers. "You're not complaining are you?"

"Not even a little bit." She giggles, watching as I store the helmet in the seat.

I snag her hand and head toward the elevator when I'm done. "So, there's a private event with the team that we can go to if you want." I scrape my fingers through my hair as I rush to continue. "It's just the players and the coaches, and some of the guys' families will be there. We have dinner and just shoot the shit. Or you can just go hang in your room and I can meet you later?" I don't want to throw too much at her, or freak her out putting her in a room with a bunch of people she doesn't know. This is supposed to be casual, but because it feels like it's more than that, I figure I'll take a chance. I want to keep spending what time I can with her because I know that's all going to change starting tomorrow. The elevator arrives and we step inside.

"What time does it start?" She presses the button for her floor, then looks at me for my floor number.

"I'll walk you to your room." I tug her up against me, my arm moving around her shoulder, my fingers toying with her braid. "It starts at seven."

She twists, pulling her phone out of her back pocket to glance at the time, then looks up at me. "Is it dressy?"

"Nope, you can show up like that if you want. Everyone is usually pretty casual." I let go of her braid as the elevator stops and the door slides open. We step out and head to her room. I release her as she unlocks the door and then step in behind her.

She shrugs the jacket off, then turns to me. "Do you want me to go? Or are you just being polite?"

I take the jacket from her hands and place it on the closest surface then draw her into my arms. "Do you really even need to ask that?" I smooth one hand over her cheek to lift her face to mine. "The next couple days are going to be all football, so I'd like to spend as much time with you tonight as I can."

"Okay, then I'll go." She offers me a small smile, her shoulder lifting. "I mean, I want to go. I really do. I just don't want to intrude or make things weird for you."

"It won't be weird at all." I drop a kiss against her forehead as I release her. "And you're definitely not intruding." I sit down on the bed and watch as she walks to the closet and starts rifling through the clothes she has hanging there. "Just be warned that some of the guys will raze the hell out of you. But also know that it's about me, and has nothing to do with you at all."

She yanks her t-shirt over her head, revealing a sheer black bra underneath that leaves nothing to the imagination, then flashes me a flirty grin, one brow lifting suggestively. "Then you'll just have to do everything you can to make it up to me later if they do." She tosses the shirt playfully at my head, then pulls a black shirt off one of the hangers, sliding it over her torso before I can get up and take advantage of her.

"With pleasure." I wink as she walks into the bathroom. I raise my voice so she can hear me as I continue talking. "So, tomorrow and Sunday, things start to get really crazy. I don't know how much time I'll actually get to spend with you."

She leans her head out the door, her fingers pulling apart the braid in her hair. "I can keep myself busy. I'm a big girl."

"Okay, I just don't want you to think I'm blowing you off." She disappears from view as she moves from the doorway. "I've got a light practice tomorrow, then more press in the afternoon, and my family will be arriving at the hotel. We watch the NFC championship game in a private room tomorrow night, and then we've got the game on Sunday, so I'll be totally off grid as I prep for that."

She steps out of the bathroom, her hair loose now, flowing in waves down her back, and her lips shiny with gloss. "I'll be fine Jasper. Really." She toes off her sneakers, then pads over to me. "Do you need to go back to your room to change or anything?"

She moves between my legs and threads her fingers in my hair and begins brushing my locks . I'm sure they're a mess between walking on the beach and the helmet. I close my eyes and hum. "That feels really good." I snake my arms around her waist and lean my head against her chest. It's strange how such a simple act of affection can trigger self-realization. And what I realize in that instant, is that I would be content to stay right here, anywhere with her, forever. And the thought of not being able to see her over the next couple of days causes a ripple of pain in my chest I didn't see coming. Never has anything or anyone been more important than football to me. And that thought sends a whole other feeling surging through my body; fear. I slide my hands to her hip, my grip tightening as I push her away to stand up.

"Oh!" Her fingers slide off my head and her hands plant on my chest, alarm in her voice. "What's wrong?"

I stare down, her deep blue irises wide with concern as a frown wrinkles the space between her eyes. Her lips are plump, and shiny, and of course, the lower one is caught between her teeth. And even with a dusting of powder, I can still see the light freckles that are scattered over her nose and cheekbones. She's beautiful. But more than that, it's how she sees me. She sees me, and only me, for who I am, and not what I am or what I do. And holy fuck, the next thought causes my heart to gallop. I'm falling for her.

"Jasper?" Her voice is barely a whisper. "Are you okay?"

"Yeah." I look up at the ceiling and blow out a long breath to calm my heart. I pull her against me, my hands cradling around her shoulders as I lower my chin, resting it on top of her head. "The pressure of the game just hit me." Little did she realize the true meaning of my words.

"I can stay here if having me with you is too much." She murmurs.

Fuck. She thinks I don't want her with me. That's actually the problem. She's all I want right now. I tilt her head back so she's looking at me. "I want you with me." I sweep a kiss across her forehead, then step back, releasing her. "And no, I don't need to go back to my room. As long as you don't mind me keeping the jackets in your room for now."

"Of course not." She offers me one of her easy, gracious smiles then walks back over to the closet. She uses her toe to drag a pair of heels out, then slides them on. "I'm ready then."

"You look great." I grin, mentally pushing any more thoughts my feelings for her aside for now. "But I do think I've mentioned before that you look pretty good in anything."

She rolls her eyes, sliding her finger through mine as we leave the room. "You're such a charmer, Jasper Chase."

We take the elevator up this time, stepping out when it reaches our floor. The organization has rented the entire roof-top restaurant for the evening. They like to give us a stress-free night to enjoy dinner and some downtime with our friends, family and teammates. I wasn't lying to Megan when I told her the next couple days would be a whirlwind for me. I wonder if I made the right decision to ask her to stay, especially knowing I won't see her much after tonight until after the game.

If we win, we'll have two weeks to prep for Super Bowl, and I won't be able to spend any of that with her. And if we lose, well, I don't even want to think about that possibility. Losing isn't an option I even want to consider. There's no real upside for her to even be with me at this point, but she is, and I'm selfish enough to take advantage. Because I like her. And I do want to keep seeing her. Even if I have to wait another two weeks to keep doing that. And let's not even factor that we don't live in the same state. I glance over at her, and all it takes is that one look to dash away any doubts I'm having. Yep, I'm falling for her. *I'm so fucked.*

Her fingers squeeze mine more tightly as she leans into me, loud chatter greeting as we turn the corner into the restaurant, a large group of people already assembled in an open lounge area. "Don't be nervous."

"Says the lion to the lamb." She retorts on a nervous laugh.

"Let's get you a drink." I head in the direction of the bar. "A little liquid courage?" I suggest playfully.

"Yes, please." Her grip relaxing in mine just slightly.

Somehow we make it to the bar without anyone stopping us to chat along the way. Within moments we both have a drink, a glass of ice water for me and a white wine for her. "You ready for this?"

"Put me in Coach." She jokes as she takes a healthy swig from her glass.

I chuckle, adding another notch to the reasons this girl couldn't be more perfect, then pull her into the fray of madness that is my team. We spend the next hour meeting the guys I'm closest with, and she's amazing. I was a little nervous about how Doug would treat her, especially after the shit that went down between us earlier, but he was a perfect gentleman. Apparently he's reserving any and all guilt shaming for the time I've been spending with Megan just for me. And I'm fine with that. She doesn't need to deal with our internal bullshit. I make arrangements for her to sit with Doug's wife, Michelle, during the game, happy to know she'll be in good hands.

During dinner though, things get a little awkward when one of the player's wives, Ally, asks me directly if Poppy will be coming to the game on Sunday. It might not have been quite so bad if the entire table didn't go radio silent as they wait for me to respond. There might as well have been a one thousand watt spot light shining on me, considering how quickly I broke into a sweat. Poppy had a ticket. I had originally invited her to the game. But I had also called her last week and asked her not to come. Things were over. Ally was a model, just like Poppy, and they travelled in the same circle, so I understood why she would ask, but I also couldn't help but be a little pissed. Did she not notice that another woman, a different woman, was currently sitting next to me?

To say I was a little surprised when Megan answered before I could, would be an understatement. "I believe that seat has been taken." And saying I was proud as fuck that she stood up for herself, would be putting it mildly.

"Oh, I didn't realize." Of course, Ally couldn't let it go that easily, lifting her nose in the air, one manicured brow arching high as she rakes a disapproving gaze over Megan.

"Realize what?" Megan counters, her own brow rising in defense as she lifts her glass of wine to her lips.

Ally snorts like she can't believe she's being challenged. "That you were anyone special." Then shifts her focus to me. "We're never quite sure with you, Jasper."

Anger surges through me, my blood instantly boiling, my spine locking into place as I shift in my seat. How dare she try and make my date, whomever it may be, feel insecure or less than what they may mean to me? Fucking bitch.

"Well, now you know." My head snaps to my right to look at Megan, who apparently doesn't need me to defend her at all. "Maybe you can let Poppy know too." I continue to watch as Megan takes a sip from her glass, my mouth dropping open when she speaks again. "Since there seems to be some confusion."

When Ally laughs out loud, then looks back over to Megan with a smile on her face, relief sweeps over me. "Well, aren't you just a little spitfire?"

"See?" I slap a hand on the table as I let out a bark of laughter, my attention swinging to Megan. "I told you!" This of course leads me to telling the story of how we met in the lobby, and my subsequent labeling of her as a spitfire. The tension at the table diffuses by the end of my tale, but I lean over anyway, covering Megan's hand with my own as I do and whisper in her ear. "You're amazing."

She angles her head, her eyes locking onto mine, amusement sparkling in them. "Not special?"

"Amazing is way better than special."

She shrugs, her lips pulling tight as she tries to restrain her smile. "If you say so."

I scoot my chair, then brush my lips to her ear. "Let's go right now and I'll show you."

She turns her head until her lips are on mine, her breath mingling with mine when they move against them. "Let's go."

My mouth curves into a wide grin as I lean back, then stand up to address our table. "We're going to call it a night." I reach for Megan's hand as she stands, pulling it into my own. "We'll see you tomorrow."

Megan says goodnight to everyone as I pull her away, my desire to have her to myself and in my arms overwhelming any need I have to be polite. As soon as we're in the elevator, I grasp her by the nape to haul her body to mine and crush my mouth to hers. She opens on a moan, her fingers curling the fabric of my t-shirt into her fists when I sweep my tongue inside. I turn and slam her back into the wall, my need for her obvious when I grind it into her hip.

The elevator stops and the doors slide open, and I somehow manage to get us to her room and inside without severing our connection. In seconds, we're naked, both of us tearing the clothes off the other. A single second after that, my hands are under her ass as I lift her onto the desk, her legs wrapping around me as I drive into her, both of us crying out as we join. There's no tenderness between us, just primal need as I thrust into her repeatedly, her hair flying wildly each time we buck against each other. Her nails claw at my shoulders as she attempts to anchor herself, my own fingers digging so deep in her hips I'm sure there will be bruises.

I lean over so that I can capture her mouth, thrusting my hips after each word I vocalize against her lips to drive home how I feel. "You. Are. Fucking. Perfect."

She locks her arms around my neck, her fingernails digging into my shoulders to hold me in place, her hips rocking into mine as she meets each of my thrusts. "So. Fucking. Good."

Her words fuel my hunger, my hips plunging faster as I increase the speed and intensity I'm driving into her, her mouth forming an O as I feel her center squeeze around my cock. "Yes, baby! Come! Come for me!"

And she does. She lets out a long moan, her muscles convulsing around me, the strangling heat of her release triggering my own, my mind fragmenting into a million particles of dust. I clutch her body against mine as I shove myself as deep as I can, my cock pulsing as my cum shoots out in long spurts, the sound of my voice echoing against the walls as I groan out my relief.

She relaxes her arms from around my neck a moment later, and I loosen my hold as well, capturing her mouth in a kiss. I don't want to break our connection, so I slide my hands under her ass and lift, making sure to keep her pressed against me when I turn and lower her to the bed. I pull my lips away from hers so I can look her in the eye. "I'm not quite done showing you how amazing you are." I steal another kiss then speak again. "Is it okay if I stay a bit longer?"

"You can stay forever if you keep doing that to me." She giggles before I silence her with my mouth, more than happy to oblige her.

Too bad forever never turns out to be quite as long as you think it's going to be.

Chapter Thirteen

"I gotta go." His voice a warm whisper in my ear as I blink awake. I feel his lips on my ear and I turn my head until they brush my lips instead. I slide my hand up his arm, my fingers drifting over the bumps of his muscles, stopping when I reach the edge of his sleeve. I slip them under the material then wrap my hand around his bicep as I try to pull him closer to me.

"Don't even think about it." He leans back, extracting himself out of my grip, a soft chuckle vibrating up from his chest. "I have practice."

I stick my lip out in an exaggerated pout, then shift back on my elbows, shrugging so that the blanket slides down my body to expose my bare chest. "Well, if you have to go."

"You are so not playing fair." He shakes his head, his tongue swiping along his bottom lip like he's oh so hungry, and then takes a step back.

I cock my head letting my hair fall over my shoulder as I

turn on my side, bringing one hand over my breast. I watch as his eyes follow the movement of my hand, unable to hide my smile when he sucks in a breath when my fingers roll a nipple between them. "When did I ever say I played fair?" I pluck the peak again, twisting it before I release it, the tip hard as it bounces in place.

He growls, literally growls, before dropping to his knees beside the bed, his mouth latching onto my breast before I can even blink. His hands cup around my globe in a tight grip, and he sucks hard, flicking his tongue against the sensitive bud. Every swipe sends a signal straight to my core, heat pooling between my legs. My fingers weave through his hair, pressing his head into my chest as I beg for more. He sucks even harder and my hips buck off the bed from the sensation. I drag one hand out of his hair and down my body until my fingers find my center. I slide my fingers over my wet seam and start to push them inside, his lips suddenly popping off my breast, my hand flying up in surprise.

My mouth falls open in protest, my brow creasing as I watch him rise back up to his feet. "What are you doing? Why are you stopping?"

He smirks, wiping his mouth on the back of his hand. "I told you, gotta go."

I sit up, trying not to splutter. "But-"

He bends, plants a kiss on my gaping mouth, then grins. "All's fair in love and war baby." He grabs both his and his sister's jacket off the chair. "Don't ever try and beat me at my own game." He winks, then pulls the door open. "I'll call you later." And just like that, he was gone. Little did I know just how gone he'd be.

I think about finishing what I was about to start before he so rudely left, but roll over instead and grab my phone off the night stand. It's just after seven-thirty, which means it's ten-thirty on the East coast. I turn on the lamp over the bed, then hit my Facetime connection for Leah. I grin like a crazy person when I see her face pop up on the screen. I can tell by the photos on the wall behind her that she's in our living room.

"Hey Megs!" She grins back at me and waves, her brow furrowing after a second. "How come every time I talk to you, you're in bed?"

"Oh my God, Leah!" I slap a hand over my face, then drag it away, trying to reveal my best, 'I'm so ashamed face'. "I think I've had more sex in the past three days then I've had in the last year."

"Well, aren't you just a dirty little slut!" She admonishes me with affection. "And lucky too, I might add. I still can't believe you're doing the deed with Jasper Fucking Chase."

"Oh, guess what?" I sit up, a million things I want to share with her popping into my head. "I have so much to tell you!"

"Tell me! Tell me!" She bounces in place as she encourages me to spill the beans.

"I went to a sports store here yesterday to see if I could get a shirt with his name or number on it. You know, for the game tomorrow and stuff." I look at her, and she nods for me to continue. "*Everyone* knew who he was. Like, I didn't get what a big deal he was until I was in there." I let out a giddy laugh, the one that she knows is my nervous laugh. "I'm seriously dating a famous person."

"I told you that the other day." She rolls her eyes so hard they practically hit the ceiling. "I bet you haven't even googled him, have you?"

"Why on earth would I google him?" I wave a hand to dismiss the idea. "I do not want to get sucked down that rabbit hole. Just hearing what you know about him is scary enough. I don't even want to know what the hell the internet has to say. I'll make my own opinions, thank you very much."

"Okay." She gives me a little frown. "I guess I shouldn't tell you that TMZ blasted a story on the news last night about Jasper Chase and new love interest spotted at The Palm in Los Angeles having dinner."

"Shut the fuck up!" I yell, my eyes bulging out of their sockets.

"And aren't you glad I told you to wear the black dress? You looked fabulous by the way." She continues, a smug smile on her lips.

"This is so surreal." I shake my head in disbelief. "He's just a regular guy to me." I blow out a breath. "Well, not just a regular guy." I look her straight in the eye, my tone getting serious. "I really, really like him, Leah."

"Rut-roh." Her head angles in concern. "I know that look." She points at me through the phone, her voice rising as she blurts out her next question. "You like him, love him already, don't you?"

I flop back on the bed, groaning out loud. "Oh my god, you do!" I hear her yell from the phone, which is now face down on my chest. I lift it again, bringing her face into view, and nod once. She lets out a short huff of laughter. "Jesus Christ on a cracker, only you Megan Lewis. Only you would fall for a freaking famous football player."

"I've never felt like this before." I sigh. "I don't really know what I'm supposed to do."

"Well, have you talked about it with him?" Leah, ever the direct and sensible friend, gets right to the point. "You are leaving tomorrow, right?"

"Yeah." I nod, and then shake my head. "Well no, I'm not flying out until early Monday morning. But yeah, we both want to keep seeing each other, we just haven't figured out all the details yet."

"What's the problem?" She persists.

"It all depends on his schedule." I sit up again and cross my legs under me. "If they win the game tomorrow, he has that super game in two weeks, but if-."

"Super Bowl."

I stop blabbering and frown. "What?"

"It's the Super Bowl. Not Super Game." She giggles. "It's a really big deal, Megan. It's like if you were an actor and you got nominated for an Oscar."

I puff out an exaggerated sigh. "Whatever. You know what I mean." I stick my tongue out at her. "So anyway, if he has to play in that, he won't be free for the next two weeks. But if they lose tomorrow, then I guess technically he's available after that."

"And?" She raises her brows looking for more information.

"And he said we'd figure it out once one or both of the games were over, but that he wants to keep seeing me."

"Oh my God! You're totally Jasper Chase's girlfriend!" She squeals. "Wait! Does this mean you get to go to Super Bowl if they win tomorrow?"

"I mean, I don't know." I lift my shoulders. "I didn't even know what the stupid game was called. Do you think I asked him if I could go?"

"Well, if he wins tomorrow, you're asking him for a ticket, and you're taking me with you!" She orders. "So, what are you doing today? Are you seeing him?"

"I'm not sure." I frown, unable to hide the fact that I hate being here for him, but not being able to actually be here for him. "He's got a bunch of team oriented things going on today, and then the game is tomorrow. He said he's going to try and get up to see me tonight, but he couldn't promise anything. I'm sitting next to some people he introduced me to last night at dinner, so I won't be alone during the game."

"Well, that kind of sucks." She points out the obvious. "So, you're just going to wait around in limbo?"

"I mean, I'm going to go do some sightseeing today. I want to go see the Hollywood sign, and thought I'd go see all the sidewalk stars on Hollywood Boulevard. You know me, I'll find a way to keep myself busy." I slide off the bed to walk over to the desk and lift the pass he gave me to show her. "And look, I have a VIP pass. I can go down onto the field after the game if they win, and it lets me into the private area that the players will be in after the game so I can meet him."

"Well, that's kind of cool." She laughs. "Too bad it's being wasted on someone who is clueless about football. Do you want me to give you an overview of the game basics?"

"Oh my God, yes!" We spend the next half hour gabbing as she explains the rules of a football game so I won't be completely lost tomorrow. I'm grateful for the lesson, but even more so for her friendship, and tell her that as we hang-up. I drag my ass to the shower after that, and do as I promised her I would, and get myself ready so I can go out and explore some of Los Angeles. I don't get back to the room until close to seven that night, and am a little disappointed I haven't heard from Jasper yet. I decide to order dinner up to my room instead of going out, in hopes he may show up, but the only thing I end up getting is a text from him after eight.

Ran into some complications and won't be able to make it tonight. Will text you tomorrow. Hope you had a good day. Miss you. Xo

I don't even text back. I know it's childish, but I guess I don't understand what could be so complicated he can't come up and see me before he goes to bed. He is the one that asked me to stay. Why am I here if he's not even going to be able to spend any time with me? I feel stupid about the choice I made to stay, and am definitely wondering if I made the correct decision. So, of course, I do the one thing I told myself I wouldn't. I grab my laptop out of my bag, fire it up and open a google window. My fingers hover above the keys as I have an internal debate with myself about the fallout of what I'm about to do. Reason doesn't seem to be a factor in my decision making however, and before I can stop, I type in 'Jasper Chase' and bang the enter key.

The first two things I notice; he has his own freaking website and for Christ's sake, a damn Wikipedia page. I am so in over my head. I click on the Wikipedia link because that seems to be the safer option. His birthday is in May, and he's thirty years old, and oh look, he went to Kent State. Shit. I roll my head back and frown. I shouldn't be finding out things like this about him on the internet. This is all stuff I want to find out organically. I bring my attention back to the screen and decide to click on images instead. That's got to be safer, right? Holy fuck. There are thousands of pictures of him. So many of him in uniform and with his team, but as I scroll further down the page, I start to see him at events. I freeze when I lock onto a picture of him dressed to the nines with a beautiful woman on his arm. Of course, because it's like watching a train wreck and you can't stop yourself, I click on the photo.

The caption alone triggers my heart to start hammering in my chest. "Model Poppy McAdams and NFL Star Jasper Chase Heating Up." The date of the article is from October. It's January. So at least the article is somewhat dated. I stare at her though and can't help but notice the similarities between us. I mean, she's a smoldering super model, she even has that frosty look down as she stares into the camera with pursed fish lips, so we're not really comparable. But she has long blonde hair, and blue eyes, and even though she's thin, she's got boobs. I look down at my chest and then back at the picture of her. I scoff. At least I know he has a type.

I don't bother reading the article. I've seen enough and slam the laptop shut, chastising myself in the process. "Stupid girl." I knew I shouldn't have opened this can of worms. I toss the laptop on the bed and decide to run a bath to try and soak away my bad attitude. The food arrives as the tub is filling, so I put it aside to eat after. I lounge in the bubbles for over thirty minutes, then shave all the places that need it, and change into Jasper's t-shirt that I swiped the other night. It still smells like him, and if he can't be here, at least I can enjoy a little part of him instead. A few hours later, I drift to sleep, still holding out hope that he might show up.

When I wake the next morning, the first thing I do is grab my phone, and smile when I see two texts from him. I swipe the first one, which he sent around eleven, and smile.

Missing your hair tangled in my hands as I kiss you. Sleep well. XO

I mean, what kind of rough and tumble football player sends a message like that? The ice that had started to form around my heart melts. I laugh out loud when I read the next text, sent just a few minutes later. He's taken a picture of Doug asleep in the bed beside his, his mouth hanging open.

And he wondered why I stayed in your room the last few nights?

At least I know he was thinking of me last night, which does wonders for dismissing the doubts I was starting to have. I need to remember he's a professional athlete and he is here for a huge game, and not to cater to me. I glance over at the roses, now in full bloom, on the desk across the room, and smile. He definitely had done more than most in the few days we've been together, even though he's got other, very important priorities. I shake off my the shitty attitude I had the night before and get up, excited to start the day. I decide to text him back, hoping maybe he'll be awake.

Good morning. Missing you, but wanted you to know I was thinking of you and hope you have a great game today.

My heart leaps when almost instantly he replies.

Morning beautiful. Thinking of you too. Find me after the game. Can't wait to hold you again.

If my heart was leaping before, it's doing fucking somersaults now. I press the phone to my chest, hugging it like it's him, a wide grin splayed across my face, and let out a short squeal of happiness. Today is going to be an amazing day.

I grimace, my hands flying to my mouth when Jasper is slammed from behind, the football popping out of his grip, flying into the air, and then into the hands of a player on the opposing team. The other player looks down at the ball, his eyes popping wide for just a second before he reacts, his legs pivoting then pumping as he runs toward the end of the field. Seconds later, that same player is spiking the ball onto the field in the end zone as he scores a touchdown. But I don't see that part. I can't tear my eyes away from Jasper as he struggles to stand, his teeth clenched in obvious pain as he limps off the field.

When he reaches the sideline, he takes his helmet off and throws it against the bench, obscenities floating across the field that reach even my ears. I'm not sure if he's pissed or hurt, but either way, I'm worried. I barely know a thing about football, but even I can tell he hasn't played well. The guy throwing the ball has aimed it for Jasper over twelve times, and he's only caught it twice. The score isn't good either. It's 24 to 7, and there are only four minutes left in the entire game.

He doesn't play any of the last four minutes, because he's led off the field by two men in suits. I'm assuming team doctors? He's limping, but he brushes any attempt at help away with an angry swipe of his arm to both men. I turn to Michelle, Doug's wife, whom I met last night. "What should I do?"

She offers me a small smile. "It depends on the injury. If they think he tore something, they may try and x-ray him. I don't think they'll take him to the hospital, even if he is injured. They'll most likely wait and have him checked out back in Boston."

I nod, ingesting her words. "Should I go down there then?"

"Wait a few minutes." She pats my arm. "I'll go down with you after the game is over. I've been through this a few times and can steer you in the right direction."

"Okay, thanks." I sit back down in my seat to wait. Which isn't very long. The rest of the game is over within twenty minutes, the Patriots losing. I follow Michelle as she weaves her way through a maze of endless hallways and people, grateful to have her guiding me. When we reach the secure part of the facility, we show our badges and our waved through without an issue. We walk down an incline that widens to an open area where many of the family members are already waiting. I'm surprised when I spot Jasper, already showered, in the far corner of the space. I'm about to call out to him, but my words catch in my throat, my smile evaporating as I watch his arms slide around none other than Poppy McAdams.

I stop in my tracks, my mouth hanging wide as I continue to watch the scene unfold in front of me. Her arms wrapping around his shoulders, her face burrowing into his neck, his eyes closing as his head leans against hers. What in the actual fuck? He said she wasn't coming. He said they were over. That sure doesn't look like the actions of a man who is over anything. I feel like a complete and utter fool.

Michelle notices that I stopped and twists around to see where I am. "Megan, you coming?" I shake my head, my eyes staying laser focused as I continue to watch Jasper hold Poppy. I'm waiting for him to push her away. To see if this is some kind of mistake, but so far, that's not happening. Michelle turns to follow my gaze, then swings her head back to me, her eyes wide. "Oh shit."

Before she can say anything else, or try to make an excuse for Jasper, I tear my eyes away from the image now burned in my brain, and look at her instead. "I have to go." I start walking backwards, slamming into someone behind me, spinning around to apologize before turning back to

Michelle. "I'm sorry." I don't offer any other explanation, because honestly, is it even necessary?

I sprint as fast as I can away from the mistake I am now realizing I made, tears starting to spill, making it even harder to find my way out of the stadium. Somehow, I manage to escape the confines of the structure now containing my shattered heart. It's complete chaos outside, and getting an Uber to pick me up almost impossible, but I finally get one, and burst into a sobbing mess the minute I'm in the car.

"Patriots fan?" The driver asks, assuming I'm crying because they lost. He laughs at his own joke, but quiets instantly when I sob louder. He doesn't say another word to me, and has me at the hotel in thirty minutes. I go straight to my room, unlock the door, and begin throwing any items I hadn't already packed into my bag. I still when I feel my phone vibrate in my back pocket, then slide it slowly out and into my field of vision.

I know before I even look that it's going to be Jasper. Lying, fucking Jasper Chase. Too good to be true. I'm surprised to see that there are five missed texts from him. I guess I missed them as I was crying over him.

Where are you? I can't find you?

Are you here? I need to see you.

Did you get lost? Please tell me where you are so I can find you.

We're leaving soon. I have to go back with the team. I hurt my ankle, need to get it checked out in Boston.

Just talked to Doug. Please call me. We need to talk. I can explain. Boarding plane in thirty minutes.

I throw the phone on the bed. Fuck you Jasper. I don't need to hear you tell me what I already know. I scream at the top of my lungs, then flop back onto the bed. I'm so mad at myself for falling for him, for being sucked in by his charm, and his damn perfect body. I am so much smarter than this. I sit up quickly, my eyes landing on the roses, my anger flaring at the very sight of them. I push off the bed, swipe them off the table, then walk into the bathroom. I hurl the vase at the shower wall, the glass shattering as it makes contact, the roses cascading into the tub in a messy heap. "Fuck you." I'm whispering, trying to fight back the tears with the betrayal I feel. "Fuck you, Jasper Chase."

I spin on my heel, close my suitcase, then grab it and my laptop bag, and leave the room. I check out of the hotel, then get a car to the airport. I'm lucky and am able to get a seat on a ten o'clock flight back to Boston. I board when my section is called, looking ahead as I enter the jet way, wanting to forget Los Angeles and everything that happened behind me.

Chapter Fourteen

Three days later...

I jerk awake, rolling over at the same time, my arm landing on a soft body sleeping soundly next to me. I groan, close my eyes, wishing all the mistakes I've made in the last few days will fucking disappear when I open them again. They don't. My head is fucking pounding, and Poppy is still laying in the bed next to me. I toss the covers back with little disregard for her comfort, and drag my ass out of the bed. I look down and notice I'm naked. I glance over at Poppy and take in her naked form, and put two and two together. Great. Just fucking great. Like I haven't fucked things up enough already, it looks like I took it to whole new level.

I barely remember what I've done since leaving Los Angeles and landing here in Boston. After I left the hospital, my ankle in an air cast while it heals from a bad sprain, I came home to find Poppy waiting for me. After the surprising news she sprang on me in Los Angeles, it felt wrong to turn her away, so I invited her in. I remember downing two pain-killers with a bottle of tequila, but after that, not much at all. I rummage through the clothes scattered across the floor of my apartment, and finally find my phone. Miraculously, the battery isn't dead, but when I see the date, and realize I've been off the grid for three days, it's a shock I'm not dead as well.

I take a seat on my couch then open my texts, scowling when I don't find one message from Megan. I open my history and see that I've sent her plenty though. God fucking damn it. I have so completely fucked this up. I double check to see what actual day it is. Yeah, that's when you know you're a mess. I shake my head when I see it's Wednesday and realize again how bad of a corner I've painted myself into. It's almost eleven, and even though I know she's probably working, I try calling her anyway. I'm not surprised when she doesn't answer, but I'm definitely disappointed. I leave a message, the last one I'll bother her with, and hope for the best.

"Hi, it's Jasper. I know I owe you an explanation, and several apologies, and really hope you'll call me back." I let out a sigh then continue quickly so the message doesn't shut down on me. "I like you Megan. I really, really like you and I want to try and make this work. Please call me. I won't bother you again if you don't, but I'm begging you for just one conversation so I can try and explain."

I drop my throbbing head into my hands, snapping back

up when I hear Poppy's voice. "Don't you think it's kind of in bad taste to call another woman when I'm still naked in your bed?"

I shake my head, a long, tired sigh sounding from me as I stare over at her. "What the hell happened, Poppy?" She's still naked as she saunters over to me, and I'm relieved when my dick doesn't even twitch. At least some things are working the way I want them to. She stops when she reaches me, then weaves her fingers into my hair and begins to stroke my scalp.

"Don't." I swat her hand away as I stand, pissed that I'm still naked too, not wanting her to think it's an invitation. Everything that has happened in the last three days has been a mistake and I need to make sure she knows that. "I told you already that this thing between us is over."

Her eyes squint in anger as she assess me, then soften as she tries to convince me otherwise. "That's not what it felt like last night, or the night before." She steps back into my space and tries to place her hand over my heart. "You said you'd take care of me, Jasper."

I sneer and step away, heading back to my bedroom so I can put some clothes on. "I don't remember anything Poppy, including what I might have said to you." I reach my dresser and pull out a pair of sweats and yank them on. I have to lean over to work the end around the cast on my leg, and stand up straight again when it's fixed. "But I can assure you this is over." I point a finger to her and then me. "This thing that you think is happening between us, isn't." I walk over to the pile of clothes and snag her dress off the floor tossing it to her. "Put something on. I'll make some coffee and we can talk about how you want to handle things."

She glares at me as she tugs the dress over her head, stomping behind me as I walk to the kitchen. "You can't just dismiss me. You're going to have to deal with this."

I spin around, grabbing my head when it throbs in protest at the quick action. I grit my teeth through the pain, then unclench them when it passes so I can continue. "I already told you that I'd be there for whatever you need from me, but we're done. I don't love you, Poppy. I'm not going to pretend I do, and this isn't going to change that."

"It's because you're in love with her, isn't it?" She plops down onto a stool at the breakfast bar, her voice laced with venom. "That girl you met in California."

"Yes!" I startle her when I respond with a raised voice. Then I still, finally admitting to myself that, even though I didn't think falling in love with someone in three days was possible, it was. I nod my head slowly, confirming in a low voice what I just realized. "Yes, I'm in love with her."

She scoffs and shakes her head. "She'll never want you after this."

I stare at Poppy, no longer sure what to say, because even though I hate to agree with her, I know she's probably right.

I stop in the hallway, just a few feet from the conference room I'm headed to for my eleven o'clock meeting, my eyes glued to the screen when I see who's trying to call me. I've gotten twenty texts from him in the last couple days, but this is the first time he's tried to call me. My finger lingers over the screen as I ponder taking the call, but then, my sanity returns and I send it to voicemail. I will not do this right now. Not when I'm about to walk into a meeting. It took me two days to even get out of bed and to stop crying over him. It's my first day back in the office and I'm going to be strong.

That strength lasted the entire length of the meeting. We just finished, and I need to go out and grab something for lunch. I decide to leave the building and run to the shop down the street for a sandwich, but I know it's just an excuse I'm using so I can listen to the message he left me. I miss him. His voice. The way he made me feel. Doesn't he at least deserve me hearing him out to see if there's a plausible explanation? After bundling up in my jacket and scarf, I head out of the office onto the bustling New York sidewalk that I love so much. I turn left and head to a café one block down that always has soups that I like, sliding my phone out of my pocket so I can listen to the message he left me.

I'm just about to hit listen when my eyes happen to snag onto a picture of Jasper on the cover of a tabloid magazine. It's hanging from one of the street vendor carts that always clutter the sidewalks, but honestly, usually don't pay attention to. I walk closer so I can read the headline, and almost choke when I feel bile rise in the back of my throat. It's not just the magazine I happened to see, it's four others, all splashed with photos of him and Poppy walking into some club, him throwing back a shot at some bar with her arm thrown around him, and the worst one, a picture of him kissing her up against some wall, snow falling around them. Headlines vary, but they all scream how Jasper is drowning his sorrow or finding solace in the arms of Poppy McAdams after the Patriots loss and his injury. He looks wasted in all of them. His eyes blurry, his face puffy, his clothes a mess. Except for the one where he's kissing her. In that one, he just looks satisfied. Mother fucker. I was actually considering listening to what this bastard had to stay.

"You gonna buy that?" The irritated vendor asks me gruffly. "This ain't the public library. You can't just check things out."

I shoot him a wary glance and shake my head. "No, I don't need this shit." I walk away before he can say anything else. My phone beeps, reminding me that it's still in my hand, and I look down, a text message from Leah popping on my screen. I can only see the beginning of the message, but I can see she's checking on me. She's worried about me. She's been amazing the last couple days, letting me vent and cry and carry on in whatever way I needed to process my feelings. I unlock the phone, then frown when it opens to the voicemail screen. A reminder that I was just considering listening to his message, and was actually considering forgiving him.

My fingers squeeze around the phone as anger grips me, and without thought, I hurl the phone against the brick wall of the building I'm passing. "Asshole!" Several people pass around me, tossing me worried glances, but not one person stops to ask if I'm okay. It's New York. Nothing surprises anyone around here. For good measure, I go over to my phone, now lying on the ground, and I stomp on it twice, the action surprisingly satisfying as it crunches under my foot. "Fuck you." I mutter, kicking the phone into the alley, as I storm away, thinking I've actually accomplished something.

Of course, fifteen minutes later when I calm down, I realize what I've done and cringe as I think of every contact I had in that phone and try to remember the last time I backed up to the cloud. I'm not the best when it comes to stuff like that, and find out later that night when I get home, that I was really bad at it. Turns out that I hadn't backed my phone up in over three months. The good news was that I no longer had any access to Jasper. The bad news was that I no longer had access to Jasper. Leah convinces me to make this permanent, thinking I'll be better off if he can't contact me either, and talks me into getting a whole new phone number when I replace my phone. A clean break, no more floundering over him. And I know she's right. It really is for the best. That is, until ten weeks later.

"What do you mean, you're pregnant?" Leah's brow scrunches up as she tries to comprehend what I've just told her. "How?"

I lift a single brow and cock my head. "Really?"

"I mean, who?" Her eyes widen as she thinks about it. "No fucking way!"

I bob my head once. "Yep."

"But it's been almost three months." She scratches her head. "You haven't slept with anyone else since him?"

I shake my head. "Nope." *And it's been exactly ten weeks and four days, but who's counting?*

"Wait, what about that guy you left the club with a few

weeks after the one who shall not be named screwed you over for Miss Poppy Pants?" She points a finger at me like she's discovered something I haven't already considered.

"I didn't sleep with him. We just made out." I shrug, not quite sure I believe what I'm about to actually say. "It's Jasper's." Before she can try and come up with other alternatives, I stop her. "There hasn't been anyone since him, and no one for at least three months before him."

"Well, shit." Her mouth hangs open a minute before she snaps out of her shock. "Are you going to tell him?"

"I don't have his number anymore, remember?" I hold up my phone in case she needs a reminder.

"Double shit." She taps her finger to her chin a few times, then stops. "You can try and message him on social media. He has a really active Instagram account. He might actually check his IM's there."

"How do you even know that?" I roll my eyes, not really needing her to answer.

"I may be secretly stalking him every now and then." She holds her palms up as she tries to defend her actions. "I just wanted to see how long it took for him and that McModel bitch to implode."

"Leah." I attempt a chastising tone, but secretly, I love that she's looking out for me.

She holds a finger up to stop me. "Hold on." She hops up from the couch, races to her room, and then is back, dropping back into her seat with her laptop. She flips it open. "Let's see if I can message him." She clicks a few buttons, then stops, her shoulders hunching together as she leans closer to the screen. "Holy shit balls." Her gaze swings over to mine, her eyes wide.

"What?" I jump up and scoot over to her, dropping down next to her, my heart stopping in my chest when I see what she's looking at.

"It's not his fucking week." She murmurs, turning to look at me, my eyes still locked on the Instagram post displayed on her screen. It's a picture of Poppy in a loose flowy dress, her hand fluttering over her stomach, the caption below stating, "Poppy's Surprise Catch! Announces she's pregnant with NFL star receiver, Jasper Chase's baby!"

"No." I whisper. My hand moving over the non-existent bump on my belly. I can't believe this is even happening. What am I supposed to do now? A wave of nausea rolls up from my stomach, and I lunge off the couch, sprinting to the bathroom, my dinner spilling out of me as I lean over the toilet.

"I'm so sorry, Megs." Leah is behind me a second later, rubbing soothing circles over my back with one hand as the other holds my braid. "What can I do?"

There's nothing left in my stomach, so I turn, sliding onto my bum next to the toilet, tears starting to trail down my cheeks. "I don't know." I take the towel she's handing me to wipe my mouth and then my face. "What am I supposed to do Le?"

She slides down onto the floor beside me and takes my hand into her own. "I don't know sweetie. This is a decision you have to make. I can't make it for you."

"I won't share this with him. With her." I sniffle then

continue. "Having to share a baby with him would be enough of a challenge, but now to try and have to figure out how to work things with her." I look over at Leah with wide eyes as I point down to my belly. "She's going to be the mother of this one's half brother or sister! Could this be any more fucked up?"

"Jesus." A gasp sounds from Leah. "I didn't even think of that."

"I'd rather just do it myself." I nod trying to convince myself I'm making the right decision. "Why would I want to confuse this baby with a father who can't seem to keep his dick in his pants and is obviously shooting his sperm all over the place."

Leah laughs beside me. "That's a little harsh, don't you think?"

I glare at her, not finding any humor in this. "It's the truth." I think back to all the times we had sex. With no condom. I trusted him. I actually thought I was special when he stuck his latex-free dick in me. "I don't need him, and I don't want him in my life. I can do this myself."

"He has a right to know, Megan." She says it quietly, knowing she's treading on dangerous ground. "No matter the circumstance, he's still the father."

"He lost any rights he had the minute he fucking lied to me." I push myself up off the floor. "I don't want to talk about it anymore." I step over her to walk away, but she grabs onto my ankle.

"Meg, you're angry right now, but that's going to change." She sighs underneath me. "I know you loved him, but keeping this baby a secret from him isn't just going to punish him, it's punishing the baby too. Just think about it, okay?"

"Uh-huh." I yank my ankle out of her grasp and storm away, knowing one hundred percent that I'm not changing my mind about this. Ever.

Chapter Fifteen
_____

Present day...

I give a final wave as I step away from the podium at the front of the room, then make my way over to the steps leading off of the stage. I've just completed the last presentation required of me at my company's annual conference, and could not be more relieved. It's been a grueling four days of interaction as I tried to impress present and hopefully new clients with our products, and now I'm looking forward to some much needed downtime.

I weave my way out of the room as quickly as I can, only being stopped twice along the way to answer questions, heaving a sigh of relief when I reach the exit doors and push through them. I head in the direction of the elevators, my heels echoing across the tiled lobby floor when I hear my name being called.

"Megan?" I'm not sure if I'm the Megan in question, so I

plant the toe of my shoe and spin in the direction of the voice. I freeze in place when my eyes connect with the person calling out my name.

"Megan! It is you." My heart rate accelerates, my pulse thundering in my ears so loud I can barely hear what he says next. "I almost didn't recognize you with your short hair." He's reached me now, and I still haven't uttered a word. I just stare at him in complete shock, a frown tarnishing his perfect lips as he points to himself. "It's Jasper. Please tell me you remember me."

I finally gather my senses and offer him a smile. "Of course I remember you." I lean forward, my fingers gripping his bicep in a loose hold as I brush an awkward kiss against his smooth cheek. I've never been this close to him when he's clean shaven. "I was just surprised to see you."

His hand sweeps against the blunt ends of my locks, just grazing the top of my shoulders. "Besides the hair, you haven't changed a bit." My hand releases his arm as I step back, my eyes fixating on his as my brain tries to catch up with my pulse. "What are you doing in Boston?"

"I'm here for a conference." I swing my gaze around the room, trying to find an exit strategy. "What about you?"

"I'm in town for the marathon. I'm supposed to meet a couple of the guys for lunch." He shakes his head, sweeping a hand over the broad smile that's lighting up his face, like he's trying to either hide or contain his joy. "I can't believe it's really you. What's it been? Three years?"

"Three and a half." I respond immediately, knowing exactly how long it's been. "Look, Jasper, I have to run, but it was lovely seeing you."

His brow creases at my obvious attempt to cut things short, not giving me the satisfaction as he tries to extend our reunion. "How long are you in town for? Do you want to have dinner tonight and catch up?" He glances for a moment at his feet, which are shifting back and forth in place, then continues. "I've wondered about you a lot over the years." He meets me in the eye, his tone becoming quiet. "There are things I'd like to say. Things I'd like to explain."

My heart catches in my throat as I swallow down the feelings lodged there. I force a small smile to play on my lips. "Unfortunately, I'm heading up to my room now to gather my things and check out."

"Can I convince you to stay?" His palm is against my cheek before I can react, the memory of his skin against my own sending a jolt of pain to my very core.

I take a step back, his hand falling to his side as I shake my head. "I'm so sorry." I retreat another step. "I already have an obligation that can't be changed."

"Oh." His brow creases again as his lips curve downward. "Well, are you still in New York? I really would love to see you now that I've found you again."

"I really don't think that's a good idea." I walk away from him, trying to be as polite as I can without breaking into a run in an attempt to escape. "I'm sorry, but I really do have to go."

Unfortunately, he's not giving up that easily, and follows after me. "Megan, wait."

I pause mid-stride, closing my eyes in the hope that I can erase what's happening right now, opening them when I feel his hand wrap around mine to stop me. "Did I do something wrong?"

I turn to meet his eyes; his beautiful, unique eyes, and respond in a whisper. "No."

"Are you married?" He glances down to my hands, bare of any rings, then back to my gaze.

I can't help the short guff of laughter that tumbles from me at the irony of his question, releasing his hand. "No."

"Then what is it?" He pleads, wanting answers that I don't want to give. That I can't give. Not now. It's too late. Too much time has passed and I know he'll be so angry.

"Momma!" A voice I know better than any other calls excitedly from behind me, spiking the anxiety I was already feeling into near panic. Goosebumps prickle over every inch of my skin as I realize what's about to happen. Little arms wrap around my legs seconds later in a hug, his sweet voice muffled against my thigh as he says Momma again. I'm frozen like a deer caught in headlights, unable to look away from Jasper as his face displays several emotions in a row; surprise, shock, confusion, and then anger as they find mine again. I lift my son to rest him on my hip, his eyes a mirror image of the man staring at us both, realization dawning across his features as his fingers splay over his gaping mouth.

In that same moment, my mother appears beside me, a little out of breath, but not so much that she can't chastise the boy in my arms. "Bennet Montgomery Lewis! How many times do I have to tell you not to run away from Grandma like that?"

Jasper's wide eyes ricochet to mine. "His name is Bennet?"

"What's going on?" My mother's head snaps back and forth as she tries to understand what's transpiring, a gasp bursting from her when she sees the resemblance between Jasper and Bennet. I nod, blinking rapidly to try and stop the tears threatening to spill from my water-rimmed eyes.

"That's a great question." Jasper's voice is low, anger seething from him as it lowers even further as he leans forward so only I can hear him. "What the fuck *is* going on?"

I clear my throat, trying to gather my thoughts, then shift my body so that I'm facing my mother. "Can you take him? Maybe back to the room or the pool?" I transfer Bennet off my hip and extend him toward my mom, her eyes still wide with shock. "I need a little while."

"Of course." She nods, Bennet wrapping his arms around her neck as she takes him. "Will you be okay?"

"She'll be fine." Jasper answers for me, startling all three of us as our heads turn in his direction. A bolt of panic jars through me when he takes a step closer to my mom, his hand reaching out to gently lift Bennet's face to stare at him. His hand slides up to cup his little cheek before moving to sweep through his sandy locks. There is no denying that he's his son. He's a miniature clone of Jasper. A constant reminder of the few days we shared together years ago, and the love that came from that time.

When he steps back, his head is shaking slightly back and forth, his eyes staying locked on Bennet for a few more seconds before they shift to me. "How could you keep him from me?"

I rip my gaze from his to address my mother. "Mom?" She seems paralyzed, wanting to know the answer as well. I've never told her who Bennet's father is, and I know she's just as eager to hear my explanation. "Please?" I urge her to leave with a look. She closes her gaping mouth, nods, then scurries away.

As soon as she's out of ear shot, Jasper asks the question he already knows the answer to. "Is he mine?"

"He's mine." I fire back. I step closer to him, wanting to show him that I'm not afraid of him or the conversation we're about to have. "And that's the way it's going to stay."

"Are you fucking kidding me right now?" He grips onto one of my forearms, pulling me even closer, his face just inches from mine as he glares down at me. "I have a son, and you think you're going to keep me from him." He scoffs, shaking his head as he continues. "You obviously don't know me at all."

I yank my arm out of his grip, pulling away from him. "I figured you already had your hands full with one baby, why confuse matters?"

"What the hell are you talking about?" Confusion mars his face.

"The baby you had with Poppy." I spit back, her name on my lips a poison I can't bear to taste.

"You don't know." He drags a hand through his hair, the strands sticking up in a thousand directions before he grips the back of his neck, his mouth creasing in a tight line as he stares at me. He lets out a short scoff. "You really don't have any fucking idea."

"Jesus Christ, Jasper." I huff out, my patience at an end. "What don't I know?"

He opens his mouth to speak, then stops, both of our heads turning when someone calls out his name. "Shit." He looks back at me. "It's Doug and Tom." He shuffles in place as he glances at them and then back at me. "We're supposed to have lunch."

"So, go." I'd be more than happy to end this conversation right now.

"Yeah, I don't fucking think so." He sneers. "I'm not letting you out of my sight until I have some answers." Before he can say anything else, the two men approach, smiles and handshakes exchanged between them.

"Holy crap, it's you, isn't it?" Doug gapes at me, then looks to Jasper for confirmation. "Los Angeles. Three years ago?"

Doesn't anyone keep track of time around here? I nod my head, then force my lips to turn up into a smile. "Three and a half actually."

"You sure did a number on my boy here." He chuckles, swiping a hand over his face as he shakes his head. "He sulked around like a dog who lost his favorite bone for months after we left Los Angeles." He delivers a soft punch to Jasper's bicep, which is returned with a dark, menacing look that clearly indicates he should shut the hell up. Doug's humorous expression changes to one of confusion in two seconds flat.

"God fucking damn it." Jasper seethes under his breath,

then looks at me. "I'll be two minutes." He takes a step away from me, then stops. "Don't go anywhere."

I nod, knowing that even if I tried to leave right now, I wouldn't get far. And honestly, because I have been dreading this moment every day since I found out I was having his baby. Maybe it would be a relief to finally get this over with. It was a moment that was going to happen at some point. If not driven by chance, Bennet would have pushed at some point to know who his father was. I watch as Jasper speaks to Doug and Tom, telling them who knows what, my mind still reeling.

A moment later, Jasper is at my side, his friends heading in the opposite direction. "Let's find some place we can talk." It's not a question, but a demand, his hand landing on the center of my back as he propels me forward.

I surge against his touch, increasing my pace as I lengthen my stride until his hand falls away. I head to a hallway off the lobby. "How about the bar? It should be quiet this time of day."

"Sure." He's increased his gait, his body now in line with mine again. "I could use a fucking drink."

I walk to a table on the far end of the room, slide into one of the chairs, and watch as he sits across from me. I want to hate him. I want my heart to remain a block of ice. But as I look at him, I already feel myself begin to melt. It's the caramel colored eyes with green flecks, the dimple in his left cheek, and the light sandy hair surrounding a face so beautiful, and so like our child's, my breath hitches in shock. My hand flies to my mouth as I feel the wall I built around my heart splinter, fissures of pain bleeding through the cracks as I finally admit the mistake I've made. I don't wait for him to talk. I just start. "I'm sorry." I know it's not enough, and I know it's too late for that, especially when I see the way he's looking at me.

"You're sorry?" He repeats, so much contempt in his voice. "You had a baby. My baby!" His hand balls into a fist as he sets it on the table. "There's no excuse for not telling me that. None!" His fist pounds against the surface once, my body flinching at the impact.

"You were having a baby with Poppy. We were practically strangers. I didn't want to confuse things." I wrench my fingers together in my lap, looking down at them as I lower my voice as I admit the last thing. "I was so mad at you for choosing her."

"I never chose her." A puff of air blows from him as he chuckles, although not one trace of humor is evident. "It wasn't my baby."

My head snaps up. "What?"

"The baby. Poppy's. It wasn't mine. I didn't find out until after the baby was born." He throws his hands in the air. "Looks like I got fucked all the way around here, doesn't it?"

Before I have a chance to react, a waitress appears, her demeanor way more cheerful than this occasion calls for. "Heya guys! I'm Chrissy. Starting the party early today, huh?"

Jasper and I exchange a look that definitely says otherwise. And it apparently doesn't go unnoticed by Chrissy, who instantly downshifts her mood into something slightly more somber. "So, yeah, okay, do you two want something to drink, or a menu?"

"I'll have a beer." Jasper orders in a clipped tone. "Whatever IPA you have on tap is fine." He looks over at me, extending his hand in my direction. "You want a glass of champagne? Maybe a bottle of Veuve for prosperity." His face is void of any emotion, but it's quite clear to me he's not being funny.

"I'll just have an ice water please, with lemon if you have it."

"Sure." She writes down our order on a pad, and I can't hide my annoyance at her continued presence and start drumming my fingers on the table. Is a glass of water and a beer that hard to remember? Her eyes dart to the noise, and then up to me, her brows shooting up as she finally gets the message. "Uh, yeah, okay. I'll be back." And then she scurries away.

I turn and zero in on Jasper, picking up where we left off. "What do you mean, the baby isn't yours?"

"It's not mine." His lips purse into a tight line as he scrapes a hand over his chin. "I found out about two months after she was born." He looks me directly in the eye. "It was a girl. Did you know that?" He shakes his head, dismissing whatever thought is in his head, and continues. "I guess I wasn't the only one that Poppy was with, and after the baby was born, her conscience got the best of her. She told me there was a fifty-fifty chance that I was the father, and she was about ninety percent sure I was, but all it took was one DNA test to prove that I one hundred percent was not."

"I'm sorry." I whisper.

"You're sorry about a lot of things apparently." He chuffs out angrily.

I ignore his anger and try to explain. "I just can't imagine how hard it must to have been to fall in love with a child you thought was yours, only to have it taken from you."

His eyes shoot up to mine, the pupils darker than I've ever seen them as they dilate, pure rage vibrating off of him when he finally speaks. "You're about to find out just how fucking hard it's going to be."

Chapter Sixteen

I'm not going to lie. I get immense satisfaction from her reaction to my words; her face paling as she shifts in her seat, goosebumps breaking out across the bare skin on her arms. Her voice is steady though, and no matter how her body may be reacting, she's not going to let me know she's scared. She's still a spitfire. "What the hell is that supposed to mean?" She's about to say more, but pauses, her eyes whipping to the left as the waitress approaches.

"Sorry." She mumbles as she sets down the drinks. "Just wave me down if you want anything else." And then she's gone, quick as a mouse, smart enough to know she should keep her distance right now.

Megan doesn't miss a beat and picks up right where she left off. "Is that supposed to be some sort of a threat? Do you think you can actually take my son away from me?"

"Our son." I lift the glass of beer to my mouth and chug down half of it in two gulps, slamming it back to the table.

"Don't you mean *our* son?" I watch as she physically reels back from the sting of my words. "I don't think we need a DNA test for this one, do we? It's pretty obvious he's mine."

She stares at me as she shakes her head slowly back and forth, not bothering to deny the obvious. "Yes, he's yours."

Even though I knew in my gut that he was mine from the very second I laid eyes on him, her admitting it sends a rush of emotion so strong through me, I feel dizzy. I lay my palms flat on the table in an attempt to regain some sort of balance, my heart beating like a drum as I exhale a long breath to try and slow it down. The anger fueling my blood for the last fifteen minutes dissipates, and quickly morphs into something entirely different. I have a son. I'm a father. To a child I don't even know. I snap my head up. "How old is he? When was he born?"

She offers me a small smile, one of resignation I think. Or is it defeat? I'm not sure because after all, I really don't know her anymore. Maybe I never really did. "He's a little over two and a half. He was born October thirty-first."

"He's a Halloween baby?" I ask, wanting to know everything I can about him.

"Yeah." She lets out a small laugh. "How's that for a trick or treat?" She fidgets with the napkin under her drink, ripping small pieces of paper away as she keeps talking. "He was born just after four in the afternoon. He came out screaming, but as soon as they put him on my chest, he stopped, and has only cried since if he's hungry. He was beautiful." She looks up to meet my eyes. "He had a full head of hair, and was so chubby. He was a good baby. A really good baby."

I stare back at her, a million thoughts racing through my mind as I add up all the things I had already missed. I'd never know him as baby. Rocking him in my arms, feeding him a bottle, seeing him grow. I had no idea what his first words were, or what he liked to eat, or when he learned to walk, what his favorite stuffed animal or blanket was. "How could you not tell me? Did you think I wouldn't want to know? Or that I wouldn't help you? Or want to be a part of his life?"

Her mouth puckers, her lids blinking rapidly at tears brimming. Some escape anyway, and she brushes them away with the back of her hand. Her lips relax but only to turn down in a frown as she begins to try and explain. "That day of the game, when I came down to see you, seeing you holding Poppy..." She trails off as she rolls her head back to look up at the ceiling, my brows furrowing as I remember that day too. She lets out a small huff, lowering her head as she continues. "You wrapped your arms around her. You closed your eyes and held her. Like she was a damn life preserver. After you had just spent the last three days screwing me. After telling me you weren't with her anymore." She gives a short shake of her head. "How do you think that made me feel?"

I lift the beer and drain the glass. I signal to the waitress to bring me another, then turn my attention back to Megan. "I tried calling you. And I texted you. At least twenty times. You never returned any of them. I wanted to explain."

"What was there to explain?" She throws her hands up

in the air. "The pictures I saw of you with Poppy all over the papers and magazines the days after said it all." Her cheeks flush a dark pink as she takes a sip of her water. When she sets down the glass, I can't help but notice how shiny her lips are, and for a second I forget why we're here and I just want to kiss her. She still takes my breath away and even though it's been over three years, it feels like no time has passed. *How the hell did we get to this place?* I give myself a mental shake and try to explain anyway, even though she doesn't think she needs to hear what I have to say.

"I hate myself for how I behaved in those days after the game. After losing. After I got hurt." I grimace as I recall the stupid shit I did. There was no valid excuse I could give for how I acted. How I treated her was wrong and the only thing I could do was own it. "I know I fucked up. I know I hurt you. But I also knew then that all I wanted was to make it right with you."

"Did you actually think I would want to see you after that?" She scoffs, a disgusted look on her face. "I do have some self-respect, Jasper."

"Fine." I pause as the waitress drops a new beer in front of me and swipes up my empty glass, walking away without a word. "But did that really warrant you not telling me you were pregnant with my baby?" She opens her mouth to speak, but I lift a hand to stop her. I have to at least try and explain my actions. "I know what I did, how I behaved, was inexcusable. I do." I blow a long breath out, then continue. "I just blew the biggest game of the season for the team. I hurt my ankle and wasn't sure how long it would be before I might be able to play again, and then-" I shake my head and scoff. "Fucking Poppy is out in the friends and family zone as soon as I step out of the locker room, and she picks that time to tells me she's pregnant. Like that news would outweigh all the shit of the game." I bring my eyes up to hers, hoping she can see the sincerity in them. "When you saw me wrapping my arms around her, my eyes closing, maybe I was holding onto her for dear life, cause I can tell you, it sure as fuck felt like I was drowning. But I promise you this, I never felt for her the way I did for you. I don't care if we had only spent three days together." I frown. "And yeah, I royally fucked up after that. Instead of dealing with shit, I tried chasing my problems away with booze and pills. I don't even remember what happened after I left the stadium and got on the plane back to Boston. I was blackout drunk for three days."

"Did you even care that I had left?" She asks quietly.

"What?" I'm taken back by her question. Did she really think I didn't care? "Of course I cared. If you had stayed even one more minute, you would have seen me push Poppy away. You would have seen me tell her to leave. And you would have seen me trying to find you."

"Well, it didn't take you too long to find her again." She cocks her head, her mouth quirking up in a tight line. "At least from what I could tell from the pictures I saw splashed all over the place." She huffs. "Thanks for that by the way. It was like someone was twisting a knife in my heart every time I had to walk down the damn street."

I take a few gulps of my beer. I'm stalling and I'm sure she knows it as she stares daggers at me. I made a fucking mess of things back then. "I'm sorry for that." I reach across the table to try and take her hand, but she leans back, pulling it into her lap. I lay my palm flat then drag it back in front of me, frowning. "I wish I had an excuse. A reason for acting like the biggest dick on the planet. Other than I was fucking stupid, and weak. None of it was worth it." I raise my gaze until it locks with hers. "None of it was worth losing you. It was all such a fucking waste."

"I guess we both made some bad decisions." She muses out loud, her eyes downcast as she focuses on her hands in her lap. "When I saw the pictures of you two together, it broke me." Her head lifts slowly until her eyes meet mine. "I know it was only three days Jasper, but somehow it was enough time for me to fall for you. I felt so betrayed. So angry. I actually threw my phone at a brick wall I was so mad." She lets out a chuff of laughter. "That was the end for me. I got a new phone, and decided to get a new number. I needed to erase you from my life. Every time my phone dinged with a message from you, it was like another stab to my heart. So, I got rid of all evidence of you, and tried to pretend it never happened."

"But to keep a baby from me?" I let out a heavy sigh. "I can't understand how you could do that."

"I didn't even realize I was pregnant until a few months later." She rests a hand over her belly, a small smile appearing before she frowns and looks up at me. "I was going to tell you. I didn't have your number anymore, so Leah had this idea to try and reach out to you on Instagram. That's when I found out Poppy was pregnant too." She huffs, shaking her head. "I couldn't believe it." She trails her gaze up until her eyes meet mine. I can see the pain in them. "I couldn't share this with her Jasper. I just couldn't."

I take a few gulps of my beer, my throat perpetually parched as I try and digest everything she's told me. I'm so mad. So mad that I want to reach across this table and shake the shit out of her. But if I've learned anything over the last few years, it's that actions taken in anger, only end up hurting me. I discovered that after I found out Poppy's baby wasn't mine. That loss hit me like a god damn semi-truck slamming into me. I can't go through that again. And it almost makes me want to walk away right now. Not take the chance of having him my life, because losing something like that again just might end me. But I also know myself well enough to know that I could never go through the rest of my life pretending there wasn't a piece of me out there. "I want to see him."

Her head jerks up, already shaking back and forth. "You saw him."

"Don't play games with me, Megan." My hand balls into a fist as I try and maintain my cool. "You know what I mean. I want to spend more time with him. Get to know him."

A tear rolls down her cheek, and she brushes it away, anger in the movement. I'm not sure if it's directed at me, the situation she's in, or because she doesn't want me to see a crack in her armor. "I have to think about this. I need a few days."

"I'll give you one." I state flatly. "Enough time has already been wasted. I want to meet my son." I arch a brow before she can give me another sarcastic reply. "Properly this time."

"I'm leaving." She waves a hand to stop my protest, continuing to speak. "We're checking out today. I won't be in Boston after today."

"Do you really think that makes a difference to me?" I scoff, unable to mask the frustration in my voice. "Megan, you will allow me to see my son. Because it's going to happen no matter what. If I have to hire a lawyer, if I have to hire a private detective, if I have to sue for custody, I will. He's mine too. You can't hide him from me anymore."

"Don't threaten me, Jasper." Her voice is laced with venom. "He's all I know and I'm not going to just thrust you onto him and expect a two year old to understand what the hell is happening. I'm his mother. I know what's best for him."

"And I'm his father!" I shout, my fist banging on the table again, her body recoiling as if I slapped her.

She recovers quickly, rising from the table. "No, you're someone I had sex with. Right now, all you are is a sperm donor. That doesn't make you a father."

She pushes away from her chair and moves to walk past me, but I stop her, standing as I capture her arm in a loose hold. "I am his father. The only reason he doesn't know me is because you kept him from me." I'm growling I'm so angry. "I will see my son. I promise you that."

Her eyes meet mine, her pupils dilated, the dark blue color like ice as she glares at me, while trying to wrench her arm from my grip. "Let go of me." She snarls when I tighten my hold instead.

With my other hand, I reach into my front pocket and pull out my bill fold. I drop it on the table, and with one hand, because I'm not letting go of her, I pull the clip off my money and cards, rifling through them until I find what I'm looking for. I slide one of my business cards off the table, releasing her as I hand it to her. "You have one day." Her eyes lock onto the card, then sweep up to meet mine. "Take it. It has all my contact information." She snatches it from between my fingers, then storms away without looking back. I call out, because I need to make sure she knows I'm serious. "You have one day, Megan!"

I watch until she's out of sight, then plop back into my chair, swiping the beer to my mouth, swallowing the contents in two seconds. I slam the glass down, my fingers clutching it's circumference, my pulse thundering in my veins. I sit there a few seconds, blowing some deep breaths in and out, startled when the waitress deposits a full beer in front of me. "Looks like you need this." She scoots away before I can thank her, both for the beer and for snapping me out of my self-pity. Not really sure what I should do next, I call the one person I hope can help me figure it out.

I reach for my cell in my back pocket and scroll through my contacts until I find the number I want, then hit call. Relief floods through me when I hear the voice answer on the other line. "Hey love bug!"

I smile, her endearment for me a comfort I didn't even know I needed. "Hey mom. You busy?"

"Never for you." The tone of her voice changes to concern. It's funny how mothers can sense, even through a phone call, when their children are in trouble. "What's wrong?"

I blow out a long breath, then dive in, telling my mom

everything. I start with running into Megan, finding out about the baby, to the time we spent together four years ago, then back to the fact that I have a baby again. After she revels in the fact that she's finally a grandmother, I express my biggest fear to her. "Mom, what if she won't let me see him?"

"She will." There's a very slight pause before she continues. "She's scared right now. Her whole world just got turned upside down."

"Her world?" I bark. "What about my world?"

"Jasper, here's the first rule of being a parent I'm going to share with you." I adjust the phone, nodding my head to indicate I'm listening, even though she can't see it. "Once you have a child, everything becomes about them. Your thoughts, your feelings, your needs will now come second." She lets out a breath. "And I know honey that you started to see this in the short time you were Alison's daddy." Alison, the daughter I thought was mine with Poppy, but learned she wasn't only a few months after she was born. "I don't mean to take that time away from you, but Megan has been raising this boy on her own for a long time now. His momma is all he knows. She's going to need a minute to figure out how this works for him. So it doesn't hurt him."

"So, I just sit here and wait? Waste more time that I could be spending getting to know him?" I know I'm whining, but if you can't whine to your mother, who then?

"Just give her some time to work this out in her head. Give her that. A mother can see what's good for her child, even if it's hard for us to admit it sometimes. And you're a good man, Jasper. Deep down, even though she's scared, I'm sure she knows that. You wouldn't have spent the time together that you did if she thought otherwise."

"Mom, there's this little person in the world that I made. I just want to know him. I don't ever want him to think I didn't want him."

"Such a good man." She repeats softly. "So much like your dad."

"Oh shit." My thoughts swinging to my father and what his reaction to this situation will be. My mother, always the mind reader, knows what I'm thinking without me saying it.

"He's going to be happy, Jasper. Right after he gets done being worried about you." She chuckles into the phone. "The joys of parenting. You'll see."

"I hope so." I whisper. "Thanks, mom."

I finish the call and hang up, promising to call her back with any updates. I wave the waitress over so I can pay my tab, my phone alerting me to a text message. I glance down at my screen, my brows jumping almost to my hairline when I read the words, hope blooming in my belly.

Saturday, Noon, 82345 Crest Ridge Estate, Stamford, CT. Don't be late.

Chapter Seventeen

The doorbell rings and I glance at the clock. It's twelve on the dot. I wring my hands, rise from the chair I'm sitting in, then make my way to the front door. I close my eyes, take a calming breath, and then pull the door open, my heart skipping a beat. Jesus, I forgot how good looking he is. And without the beard, he's even more handsome. He's got a dimple in his chin. I stare at it a second, realizing that Ben has the exact same dip in his as well. I had no idea because of the beard.

"Hi." His voice snaps me out of my daze. "I'm sorry if I'm early."

"You're right on time, actually." I tilt my head as I scan lower, noticing his hands are full. "And you come bearing gifts I see?"

He lifts his shoulders in a shrug. "I wanted to bring him something. But I wasn't sure what he might already have or like, so I may have gone overboard." He grins sheepishly, and I want to slap myself when I feel my stomach flutter in excitement. *Down girl! He's not here for you!*

I take a step back, and pull the door wider. "Come in."

He takes a few steps, surprising me when he stops to lean over and brush a swift kiss against my cheek. "Thank you for letting me see him."

It happens so quickly that I barely have time to react before he's moving past me into the foyer. I stand in the empty doorway for a good ten seconds as I try to rationalize how I should respond, but I come up blank. All I can think about is how good he still smells. What in the world is wrong with me? I need to snap out of this spell I seem to fall under every time he's around. I finally shut the door, then spin around to face him.

"This is-"

"Ben is-"

We both start to speak at the same time, and then both stop, waiting for the other to finish. I incline my head just a tad. "You go."

"This is a really nice home." His eyes take in the large foyer, then land back on me. "Is this where you live now?"

"No, I actually still live in New York, in the city." I force my feet to move and walk past him, motioning for him to follow me. "This is my mother's house. It's where I grew up. We already had plans to stay here this weekend, so it just seemed easier for you to come here. She's out running errands, but should be back in a little while." I stop when we reach the living room. I point to one of the couches. "You can put that stuff down there if you'd like."

I watch as he deposits the many gifts he's brought, my

eyes zoning in on the shifting muscles of his back as he bends over. Why does he have to be so damn good looking? I'm still staring when he turns around, my cheeks heating when I see one side of his mouth quirk up as he catches me. I move over to one of the built-in shelves lining the closest wall and lift the baby monitor, hoping to draw his attention to something other than my embarrassment. "Ben is asleep." I grab a photo album off one of the shelves, then walk towards Jasper. "He usually stays down until around one. I figured it would be good for us to have some time to talk."

His eyes stay glued to me as I come closer. It makes me nervous. He's being so quiet, so agreeable. My insides are trembling, but I know I have to give him the chance to be a father to Ben. It's the right thing to do. I press the album against my chest when I reach him, thinking of anything I can do to stall this a few minutes longer.

"Have you eaten? I can make you something. It is lunch time after all." I swing my head in the direction of the kitchen. "Or I can get you something to drink?" I whip my head back to him, a nervous laugh escaping. "Where are my manners?"

He startles me, my whole body flinching when his hand reaches out to wrap around the back of my neck, his eyes locking onto mine as he begins to speak softly. "Megan, please don't be scared. I just want to get to know him. I'd never take him away from you. You're his mother."

I nod, blinking rapidly as I feel my eyes water, a shaky breath falling from my lips as a wave of relief flows over me. "And, you're his father. I just--" I close my eyes, needing a second, then open them to meet his again. "I've just made a mess of everything." I offer him a sad smile. "After I left you the other day, it hit me how unfair I had been to you. And to Ben. How wrong it was for me to keep him from you. I could have found a way to tell you. I could have." I step out of his hold and shake my head, angry at myself for the tears that have started to fall. I didn't want be weak in front of him. "I'm sorry, Jasper." I force myself to look him in the eye. "So very sorry."

He stares at me, his hands balled into loose fists at his side, his feet shifting, his silence unnerving my already frazzled emotions. I wait though, and stay still as he continues to scrutinize me. After only a few moments, but what feels like an hour, he finally speaks, his voice clipped. "I want to be angry at you. I wanted to hurt you in some way. Maybe try and take Ben away from you. Make you feel what I felt the other day."

I suck in a breath of air at his confession, my hand flying over my open mouth as I take a step back. He counters and steps closer to me, his tone softening. "But after lying awake for the entire night, I realized that only hurts our child. And Jesus, how much more damn time do we need to waste being angry at each other?" He shakes his head, his hand scraping through his hair before clutching onto the back of his neck as he gazes up at the ceiling. "So much time has already been lost. I've already missed so much." He drops his hand, his head lowering to look down at me. "It's enough. I just want to move forward. I just want to know my son and be a part of his life."

I nod, because my heart is stuck in my throat and

speaking right now is impossible. I'm getting off easy. He could make this so much harder on me. Not that anything still to come will be easy. There are so many things we need to figure out, but him forgiving me, his ability to let go of his anger to focus on our son instead? It says everything I need to know about the kind of father he will be. He's already putting Ben first.

"So, what do you have there?" He points to the book I've still got clutched to my chest.

I look down, forgetting that I was even holding it. I clear my throat as I loosen my grip, extending it out to him. "It's a photo album. It's my mom's, so it doesn't have everything in it, but I figured it would be a start."

He slides the large book from my fingers, his face lighting up as he transfers his attention to it, his body moving unconsciously to sit down on the couch. He flips open the cover, and I lower myself next to him so I can walk him through the different pictures.

"That's the day after he was born." I smile at the memory as I point to the first page. It's a snap of me holding Ben in the hospital bed. I point to the opposite page. "That's my mom in that picture, and that's my best friend, Leah."

He turns his head to look at me, wonder and curiosity seeming to light up his eyes. "What was it like being pregnant with him? And having him? Was it hard for you? Was someone there with you?"

I lay my hands flat on my lap, leaning back into the couch as I try and answer all his questions. "I had a good pregnancy. I had very little morning sickness, and I don't even think I started to show until I was around twenty weeks. Labor sucked." I laugh. "Not going to lie about that. But Leah was there with me through the whole thing. She was amazing. Screaming at me to push, and to be tough. And it was all worth it when they finally put him in my arms." My voice softens. "He was the most beautiful thing I had ever seen. I didn't know it was possible to love anything so much until I held him."

"I wish I had been there." His voice, shaky, rips through my heart.

"I'm sorry." I whisper. Knowing the words do little to no good, but feeling like I need to say them again and again.

"I know." He blows out a long breath, his eyes capturing mine when he speaks. "You named him Bennet?"

I nod. "Bennet Montgomery Lewis. Montgomery was my father's name." I explain. "But we call him Ben."

"You gave him a piece of me." He stares down at the photo of me holding Ben. "Even though you kept him from me." He shifts his gaze back to me.

"I guess I didn't hate you as much as I wanted to." I shrug, not really having any other way to explain it.

It seems to be enough, at least for now, because he turns back to the album, flipping the page. "Please, tell me more."

We spend the next twenty minutes looking through all the pages as I explain each stage of Ben's young life through pictures. I'm hoping to give him some sense of who his son is, but I know it's just a small glimpse of all the experiences he's missed with him. When we close the book, I try and tell him as much as I can before Ben wakes. "He's always a little cranky and clingy when he first wakes up, so don't be hurt if he shies away from you. He's not usually good with strangers." I snap my eyes to his, the meaning of my words stinging even me as I apologize yet again. I forge on when he nods, a frown marring his face. "And he'll be hungry. I usually feed him lunch once he's up, so you can help with that. He hates sitting in a high chair, so I have a little booster seat I use for him. He can drink from a cup, but I have to watch him like a hawk, cause he'll throw it on the floor faster than you can blink."

"Does he talk?" He shifts, his hands wringing together on top of the album, and it dawns on me for the first time that he's really nervous.

"Don't worry." I don't want to send the wrong message, but I also want to offer him some comfort, so I lay my hands over his and squeeze gently. "He'll get to know you and probably won't want anything to do with me after he does." I laugh, then answer his question. "He's starting to talk. He says lots of words, and some simple sentences. No is his favorite right now." I laugh, lifting my hands off of his and settle them back in my lap. "I have no way to try and explain to him who Daddy is though." My brow furrows as I think out loud. "We're just going to have to work that out as we go, okay?"

"Okay." He nods, offering me a small smile. "I'll follow your lead on things."

And as if on cue, Ben's voice squawks over the monitor, Jasper's head snapping in the direction of the noise. "He's awake." I stand, taking the album from him as I do, moving over to the bookshelf to put it back in its place, and then silence the monitor. "You ready for this?"

He's standing when I turn around, his face a slight shade

of pale. He nods, then wipes his palms down the front of his jeans. "As I'll ever be."

I stroll by him, patting his bicep, (*damn, still hard as a rock*). "You'll be fine." I point down the hallway. "Why don't you meet me in the kitchen? It's down there. You can't miss it."

"Okay." He nods again, his hands flexing as I watch him walk off.

I head upstairs, change Ben into a clean diaper and a fresh set of clothes, then carry him downstairs. His head rests on my shoulder, his thumb stuck in his mouth when I enter the kitchen, Jasper pacing across the room. He freezes in place when he notices us, his gaze locking onto the boy in my arms.

I wave him closer with one hand. "Come say hello to your son."

He moves slowly, his hand over his mouth as his wide eyes sweep up and down the length of the small body I'm holding. He seems to be in awe of him, and another stab of guilt shoots straight to my heart as I again realize the enormity of my actions. I clear my throat, then speak in a gentle tone. "Hey baby, can you say hi to--" My eyes dart up to Jasper's as I realize I hadn't even thought about how I should address him. I'm met with a slight shake of the head and a furrowed brow, spurring my decision. "Can you say hi to your daddy?"

Jasper's standing right next to us now and he reaches a hand up to deliver a soft stroke over Ben's locks as he speaks. "Hey, Bub."

I expect Ben to burrow into me. I expect his arms to

tighten around my neck as he moans out a protest. I expect him to want me, and me only. But like everything in this dance between Jasper and I, nothing ever seems to go as expected. My breath catches in my throat when Ben's head lifts off my shoulder, and his arms leave my neck to reach out to Jasper.

Jasper seems as shocked as me, his eyes darting up to mine for guidance. I shrug, speechless, and give in to my son's wishes, transferring him into his father's open arms. I watch in awe, knowing it's the beginning of something bigger than both of us. Every moment of indecision I've had over the last three years is wiped away the instant my baby's arms wrap around Jasper's neck and I recognize the complete and utter look of love on his face. It's probably the same look I had on my face the first time I held him in my arms, and every day since then when I look at him. I take a step back and give Jasper this moment.

Chapter Eighteen

I can't believe he came right to me. That he wanted to come to me. My heart is galloping like the hooves of a hundred stallions racing across the plains. I hold him against my chest, surprised by his weight, even though he feels so little in my arms. I'm mesmerized as we stare at each other. It's like we're both measuring the other, trying to figure out who is supposed to do what first. He looks so much like I did when I was little. It's like looking at a picture of my younger self come to life. I want to press a thousand kisses to his head, one for every day I didn't get to hold him. I want him to know I'm already in love with him. That I'll always be here for him. That he's the very most important thing to me now. Instead, I just smile, because I can't help it, and say hello.

"Hey Ben."

His little eyes squint as they move to my mouth, his hand following a second after to run over the light stubble around my lips. "Fuwwy." He giggles, then drags his fingers over the growth again, turning his head to Megan. "Fuwwy, Mommy."

She's got a wide smile on her face as she nods. "Yes, he's got a furry face, huh?"

I laugh, now that I know what he was trying to say, but stop immediately when I feel Ben flinch in my arms, his expression turning to one of alarm as he stares at me. I think I scared him. "You think this is furry? Wait until winter." I chuckle, relief pouring through me when he seems to relax, both hands clamping on to my cheeks to rub up and down. I talk to him as he squishes my face. "Are you hungry? Mommy says you like lunch when you wake up."

His eyes widen, as well as his smile, as he replies. "Yum yums!" He claps his hands then looks at his mother. "Yum yums, Mommy."

"Okay, okay." She rubs his back as she turns to walk over to the fridge. "Let's see what grandma has in here for you." She looks over her shoulder at me. "You can put him in that seat over there." She motions to a booster strapped to one of the chairs at the kitchen table. "Make sure you buckle him in, okay?"

"Um, sure." I shift Ben over to my hip as I head for the chair, then lower my voice so only he can hear me. "She does know I haven't done this before, right?"

"I help!" He offers, clapping his hands together once.

"Well, alright little dude, let's do this." I sit him down in the seat, and somehow, with some actual direction from Ben, I get him buckled into the seat. I raise my hand to celebrate. "Give me five!" He looks at my hand, confusion on his face. How can this kid not know what a high five is? It's a good thing I'm here now. He obviously needs some male guidance. I shake my head, but then use my other hand to lift his and show him how to smack it against my raised one. "See? Give me five!"

I show him again, and this time something clicks, his tiny hand slamming into my large one as he yells out. "Gimme Five!"

"Yeah!" I yell back, excitement pouring through me. I taught him something!

"Settle down Champ." Megan chuckles from behind me. "Get him to go potty on the toilet and I'll give you a something to cheer about."

My brow shoots up as I snap around to look at her. "Something to aim for."

Her cheeks flush, and I'm reminded of a time that doesn't really seem all that long ago. When all I had to do was look at her to get that reaction from her. We spend the next twenty minutes feeding him. Well, watching him eat really. She gives him some sliced apples, then a peanut butter and jelly sandwich cut into tiny squares, and then one chocolate chip cookie. Which he refuses to share with me. Just watching him is fascinating to me. He is so happy. The simplest things sending him into a fit of giggles. I swear to god my heart has doubled in size since I walked through the door an hour ago.

After he finishes his cookie, Megan uses a wet paper towel to clean his hands and face, then pops him out of the chair. "Why don't you go show him what you got him?" She nods her head in the direction of the living room. "I'll just finish cleaning up in here then meet you in there."

"You sure?" I look down at Ben, who's running in circles around my legs, then back at her. "What if I do something wrong with him?"

"You're not going to break him." She waves me off. "Go. Trust your instincts. You'll know what's right or wrong."

I heave out a breath, then bend down to scoop up Ben, a yelp of joy sounding when I toss him gently in the air before securing him in my arms. "What do you say Bub, want some presents?"

"Pwesents!" He exclaims in delight, his head bobbing up and down. "I wove pwesents!"

I grin from ear to ear, never more excited to share some gifts as I carry him back into the living room. When I reach the couch, I set him down, then dump both bags onto the floor, letting him decide what he likes, or doesn't. A small thrill bursts right to my soul at the first thing he grabs, then runs over, holding it out to me. "Footbaw!"

We spend the next fifteen minutes going through everything else I brought, exploring all of it, but when we finish, he goes right back to the football. "Pway catch with me?"

Sure I'll play catch with you. Every single damn day if you want. For the rest of my life. Pride courses through me. This is my son. I'm a father. To a boy who wants to play football with me. I ruffle his hair under my hand, then sweep him up, unable to hide the tears glistening as I hug him close. His little body tenses for just a second, but then relaxes, his arms moving to wrap around my neck, one of his hands patting me on the back of the head. "Don't cwy. It's okay."

"I'm okay." I give him a little squeeze to reassure him. *So not okay. Kind of freaking out here.* "There's no crying in football, right?" I force a chuckle, then lower him to the ground, wiping away the light wetness coating my cheeks before he can see. "Let's go ask Mommy if we can play outside."

"Okay." He shrugs, stuffing the football under one arm, his free hand sliding into mine like he's done it a hundred times before. I close my eyes, willing my heart not to burst, then open them, my gaze landing on Megan.

There's an expression on her face that I've never seen before. Although, I doubt I've seen even a quarter of them yet, but I keep my eyes on hers for a full ten seconds as I try to figure out what it is. I'm not sure if it's a sense of peace, or maybe a sense of wonder. What I do know is that she looks beautiful. Before I can ask, Ben tugs on my hand, jumping in place as he pleads with Megan. "Can we go pway outside Mommy?"

"Sure." She bends down so she's eye level with him. "Can mommy have a hug first?" She opens her arms as he releases my hand and launches into her, the football crushed between them. "I love you Bugaboo."

"I wove you Mommy." His tender voice a murmur against her chest.

She releases him after just a second, then rises back to her full height. She opens her mouth to speak, but then stops, her head tilting in the direction of the foyer as a loud knock sounds at the door. She holds up a finger. "One sec." She looks at Ben, then back at me. "You got him?"

"Yep." I tell her as she head to the door, then flash him a grin. "Toss me that ball, Ben." He grips it between his hands then lobs it up in the air to me. I catch it then toss it gently back to him. We continue tossing the ball, me coaching him on how to throw it more directly, instead of the lobbing into the air motion he's mastered.

"Are we supposed to be throwing the ball in the house?" Megan teases as she walks back into the room a few minutes later.

My heart lurches when Ben drops the ball to the floor and breaks into a run, throwing himself into the arms of a man entering the room just behind her. "Unca Tom!" I'm getting used to his L's and R's being pronounced as W's, or not at all, so I figure out pretty quickly that he's calling him Uncle Tom. I also remember that Megan's an only child. I watch as he spins Ben around, both of them laughing out loud, my hands clenching into tight balls. *Who in the hell is this guy? And why does my son seem to know him so well?*

Megan must sense the shift in my demeanor, because she steps between me and *Uncle Tom* and tells him to put Ben down. She tells Ben to go play with his new toys, which he does, sprinting over to the pile, happy as a clam when he digs in. She looks at me, then looks at Tom. "Tom, this is Ben's dad, Jasper Chase." She sweeps a hand in my direction, her gaze snapping to me. "And Jasper, this is Tom Pearson."

"Hey, it's nice to meet you, man." He takes the three steps needed to close the distance between us, extending his hand to me. I unclench my fingers and grasp his hand in mine, shaking it firmly before I drop it. He continues to talk, and I continue to assess him. There's something familiar about him but I can't pin-point it. "Megs told me you would be coming by today to spend some time with Ben. That's really great."

Megs? What in the actual fuck? He has a nick-name for her. "Uh, yeah." I scratch at the stubble lining my chin. I'm not really sure what else to say to him, but it doesn't seem to matter because he keeps on talking.

"I don't know if you'll remember, but we actually played against each other a few times in college. I was quarterback at Arizona State back in the day." He frowns, glancing down at his leg, then back up at me. "Was supposed to go play for the Rams, but I guess destiny had other plans for me."

"That's right." I finally respond. "I remember you now. You had a hell of an arm. I was sorry to hear about your accident."

"Yep." He shrugs. "Sucked, but life goes on, right?" He points to Ben. "But have you seen the arm on that guy though?" He lets out a short laugh. "At least now I understand where the talent came from. It sure wasn't her." He looks over at Megan with an affectionate grin.

And at least now I know why he was so excited when he saw the football. It had nothing to do with me after all. And everything to do with this guy apparently. I feel like an interloper in my own son's life and it sucks. There's a part of me that wants to lift my leg and start peeing on what's mine, but the more reasonable part of me knows that's not what's best for Ben.

I'm about to make an excuse to Megan about leaving so I can take some time to digest this new player and figure out my next move, but freeze when a door slams and a woman's voice calls out. "I'm home!" A second later, her mom breezes into the living room, at least two dozen balloons clutched in her grip. "Hello babies!" She's looking at Megan and Tom, but then swings her attention to me. "And you too."

She walks over to Megan, hands her the balloons absently, then beelines to me, completely ignoring Tom. "So, you're the guy." She takes one of my hands and holds it between both of hers. "You're Bennet's father?"

I nod, completely caught off guard, my voice stuck somewhere between my belly and my throat, allowing me to only grunt a one word reply. "Yeah."

She openly scans me from head to toe, then nods. "Montgomery would have liked you." She squeezes my hand and then releases it, surprising me when she pulls me into a hug, speaking softly into my shoulder. "Welcome to the family, son. You can call me Sandy."

"Mom." Megan groans out. "Let go of him, and come say hello to Tom."

She releases me after one final pat on my shoulder, then spins around. "Tom! It's perfect you're here. Be a dear and go grab the rest of the bags out of the Range Rover, would you?"

"Sure Mrs. L, anything for you." He strolls out of the room.

I take this opportunity to try and make my exit. "Megan, I think I should probably get going." I glance at the huge bouquet of balloons she's still holding on to. "It looks like you've got some other stuff going on."

"No." She huffs out, forcing the balloons back into her mother's grasp as she strolls over to me. "This is all my mother." She swings her gaze over her shoulder to her mom. "I told you I did not want a party, but you never listen."

"Oh nonsense Meggie Pie!" She waves a hand in the air dismissing Megan's comment away like a pesky fly. "You only turn thirty once!"

"Yes, except my birthday is actually next Saturday, and not today mom." She grumbles out.

Shit. That's right. I do remember her telling me during the time we spent in L.A. that her birthday was in April.

"Yes, and since you won't be here next weekend, you get a party today." She turns her attention to me. "You should stay Jasper." She pauses when Megan throws her an evil glance. "What?" She rolls her eyes at her daughter then continues addressing me. "There's plenty of room here. Unless you got a hotel of course. But you're welcome to stay. I can have the caterer's set an extra place."

"For Christ's sake, Mom." She's reached me now and places a hand on my arm as she shifts her focus to me. "I'm sorry about that. About her." She tosses a glance over her shoulder, then looks up at me. "But yes, please, if you'd like to stay, we'd love to have you. It's just dinner with some of my friends. Leah's coming with her new husband. You can meet them."

"I really don't want to intrude." I look over at Ben, who is content as a fish in water, still playing with the toys I brought him. I crave spending more time with him, and this would at least give me that opportunity. "I didn't bring a change of clothes." I frown, lifting my shoulders in a small shrug. "I planned on just driving back to Boston today because I wasn't sure what our arrangement was going to be for me to see him again."

She crosses her arms, her attention swinging to Tom for a second when he strides by, arms full, heading in the direction of the kitchen. When she looks back at me, her lower lip is caught between her teeth. The memory of how I used to use my own teeth to nip it free before claiming her lips in a kiss slams into me. *God damn, what I wouldn't do to taste her again.* Before I can take the thought further, she starts to speak again, her voice low. "Jasper, I know this is really strange. It's a lot to take in. Getting to know Ben is a big enough change for you, but then to have to try and figure out my mother and my friends..." She trails off, shrugging, a knowing smile on her face. "I get it if you want to leave." She uncrosses her arms and places a hand on my chest, right over my heart. "But, I would really like it if you stayed."

Tom waltzes back into the room, coming up behind Megan, without any regard to the conversation we're obviously having, and drops a hand over shoulder. "I forgot how much your mom likes to order me around."

My eyes are laser focused on Megan's hand as it leaves my chest to move to her shoulder, landing over Tom's giving it a hug as she laughs out. "I think you secretly love her bossing you around."

A surge of testosterone surges through me, sparking the desire to throttle this guy right in the fucking face. *That's my girl. The mother of my child. Not yours. Yeah, I think I will stay a little longer.* "You know what *Megs*, I think I will stay, if you don't mind." My voice is laced with fake cheer. "I'd love to help you celebrate turning thirty." I swing my gaze to Ben. "And of course, spend some more time with my son."

"Okay." Her mouth quirks in a frown, her brow furrowing as she analyzes me, nodding once. "Do you want to take him outside to play for a little while? I'll make sure one of the guest rooms are setup for you."

"Sounds good." I give her a sly grin, then say something I know I shouldn't, but blurt it out anyway. "Sleeping under the same roof with you again will be nice." Then I shoot a glaring look at Tom in an attempt to deliver a silent message; *that's right fucker, she was mine way before she was yours.*

Chapter Nineteen

What in the world? Did he just try to mark his territory?

"What's his problem?" Tom grumbles behind me as I watch Jasper lead Ben outside through one of the French doors.

"I have no idea." I swing around to face him, taking a quick step back when I realize we're so close. "Jesus, a little space Tom."

"I thought you liked when I crowded you a little?" His voice lowers an octave as he steps close to me again, his hand trailing up my arm.

"What has gotten into you? I take another step back, swatting his hand away. "Are you for real right now?"

He crosses his arms, a frown tugging one side of his mouth down. "I thought after Leah's wedding, maybe things had taken a new direction for us?"

I roll my eyes, then cross my arms as well, mimicking his stance. "First off, I was drunk. Like really drunk. The most drunk I think I've been since before Ben was born." I start tapping my foot, unable to hide the annoyance I feel at even having to explain myself to him. "Making out with you in the coat room was…" I pause, looking for the right word. "-fun." Then I bring my eyes up to his. "But Tom, that's all it was for me. We've been friends way too long for us to try and go down this road now." I uncross my arms and throw one in the air. "Besides, your sister would blow a damn gasket if we ended up together. You know she has other plans for you."

"Juliette?" He scoffs. "That is so not happening. She's half a ticket short to boarding the crazy train. I slept with her once and she was ready to move in." He shakes his head. "Not going there." He pauses, shifts his stance, and then locks his gaze onto mine. "So, no me and you?"

"No." I offer him a small smile. "You know I love you, Tom." I shrug. "But not like that."

"Well, I think baby daddy out there thinks otherwise." He points outside where we can see Ben and Jasper running around. "What's your game plan for that?"

I give my foot a little stomp. "If I hear one more sports analogy today, I'm going to snap."

"Whoa." Tom chuckles. "Settle down there, Tiger. I was just asking. It's pretty obvious he's still got it bad for you." His brows rise. "The question is, do you still have it bad from him?"

"Are you sure you and your sister aren't twins?" I huff out, throwing my hands up. "I get enough of this from her." I move past him to head to the kitchen. "Come on, let's go help my mom."

"Fine!" He catches up to me and slings a friendly arm over my shoulder, leaning down as he speaks quietly. "But you're going to have to figure it out. Don't think you're gonna be able to hide from this one, Megs."

I scrunch my nose up, turning to flash him a look that could kill. "I don't need you to be my damn conscious, Tom. So, shut it."

He just chuckles, knowing me well enough to end this discussion before I lose my temper. And I will. Because I know he's right. Even if the last thing I want to do is admit it. Time hasn't dimmed the attraction I feel for Jasper in the slightest. In fact, seeing him with our son today, probably only added gasoline to an already simmering burn. It was taking every ounce of control I had not to throw myself in his lap so I could feel his arms around me again. To feel the warmth of his body against mine again, his mouth roving over my body in the magical way it did years ago.

"Earth to Megan." My mother is standing beside me, her raised voice dragging me out of the trance I'm in, my eyes darting to her as she continues to speak. "Did you hear anything I just said?" She shakes her head, concern lining her face. "You looked like you were a million miles away."

"Sorry, mom." I force a smile. "I was just thinking about how I should schedule time with Jasper."

"For Ben?" Her brow arches as she smirks.

"Obviously." Jesus, was I being that transparent? I need to get myself in check. "I'm going to go make sure one of the guest bedrooms is set up for him."

"The room next to yours is available." Now who's being transparent? She waves a hand when I cock my head at her, glaring. "Don't give me that look. I put Leah and Tyler in the largest room, Tom is in the room on the other side of Ben, so that just leaves the one next to yours."

"What about the room next to yours?" My hand comes to rest on my jutting hip as I challenge her.

"Oh, I've got a sewing project all spread out on the bed in there." She gives me a triumphant smile. "Sorry."

"Yeah, sure you are." I mutter under my breath as I leave the kitchen and head toward the living room. I peak outside to check on my boys. I stop in my tracks. *Shit.* My boy. Singular. Jasper is not mine. Never really was. I shake my head trying to untangle all the confusion swirling there, then continue to the stairs to go take care of my intended task.

It doesn't take long for me to put fresh sheets on the bed. I make sure to use the highest thread count sheets we have for this bed. I know it's silly, but I want to make sure he's comfortable. Since I can't be the one wrapping my arms around him, might as well make sure the sheets are soft. I peek out the window, smiling when I see Jasper pushing Ben on the swing. Seeing them together, so content, their interaction so natural, sends another pang of guilt through me. I should have told him. I should have tried harder to get in touch with him. So many things he's missed out on now. All because of me.

I stare at him, taking notice of how defined his body still is, the muscles in his thighs bulging through his jeans every time he leans forward to push the swing. Jesus, he's still hot as hell. As if he can sense me, he turns, looks over his shoulder, scans the house, stopping when his eyes lock onto me. Shit. My cheeks flame with heat as I realize I'm busted. I give a quick wave, then scurry away, leaving the room to go back downstairs.

My timing couldn't be better. The front door swings open just as my foot hits the last step, and I break into a happy dance. "You're here!"

"I'm here!" Leah sing-songs before swamping me in a hug. "Damn, I missed you girl!" She pushes me away, her eyes wide, her voice low as she starts firing questions at me. "So, is he here still? That's his Porsche, right? The one in the driveway?" I look over her shoulder, seeing Tyler first, heading our way with a suitcase, but then notice the Porsche SUV. I had no idea what he drove, but damn, that's a nice ride. I shift my focus back to Leah who's still talking. "Did Ben like him? Where are they now? Is he still hot?"

"Honey, take a breath." Tyler chuckles as he walks into the house, then looks at me. "Hey Megan."

"Tyler." I smile, moving to give him a hug, then point to the luggage. "You can put that up in the room you guys usually stay in if you want."

"Sounds good." He heads for the stairs, stopping beside Leah. "Be nice."

Her mouth drops open a quick second, her brow furrowing as she swings her head back and forth to Tyler and then me. "I'm always nice."

"Except when you're not." He chuckles, climbing the stairs. "I'm going to change, then I'll be down."

Leah's head turns back to me, a pout on her lips. "I'm nice."

I laugh. "Of course you are." God I missed her. I love

Tyler and couldn't be happier for her and the new life they have together, but I hardly got to see her anymore. Tyler's a musician, and travels a lot. And she made the decision to stop working so she could be with him on the road. They left on a tour just three days after they got married, and just got back into town a couple days ago. The good news is that they live in the city, so when they are home, at least we're close. I wrap an arm around her waist and give her a side hug. "Come on, let's go say hi to my mom."

"But you haven't told me anything yet!" She huffs out as we start walking. "I want to know everything."

"Of course you do!" I laugh, then tell her what I can in the short walk to the kitchen. "Yes, he's still here. I guess that's his car, I actually didn't look, but it's not my mom's and it's not Tom's. He's outside playing with Ben right now, and Leah, I think Net is already in love with him." I stop walking so I can turn and look at her. "He didn't even hesitate to go to him. And Jasper." I shake my head in disbelief. "He's amazing with him." I frown, lowering my voice. "I feel so shitty. Now that I've seen him with Ben. I should have told him so long ago."

Leah rolls her eyes. "I think I told you that like a thousand times." She pulls me into a hug when I frown. "Oh honey, it's okay. I know you thought you were doing the right thing then." She draws back from me, looking me in the eye. "And he's here now. So let's just focus on that, okay?"

"Okay." I smile at her. "I've missed you so much."

"Ditto." We start walking again as she continues. "I have so much to tell you. The tour was so much fun."

"So, married life is good?"

"Amazing." She's practically glowing as she beams a hundred mega-watt smile my way. "I'm so happy, Megs."

"Good." I beam back at her.

We turn into the kitchen, my mom giving a little shout of joy when she lays eyes on us. "Leah! You're here! I didn't hear you come in!" She strides over, then wraps her arms around Leah in a hug. "Now both my girls are home."

"Awe, Mrs. Lewis, you're going make me cry." Leah blinks her glistening eyes as they pull apart.

"Happy tears are the best kind." My mom places her palm on Leah's cheek affectionately, a warm smile on her face. "You look good. Marriage agrees with you." Before Leah can reply, my mom drops her hand and swings back in the direction of the counter. "So, where is that husband of yours?"

"I'm right here." His deep voice sounds as he enters the room. "And look who I found!" He looks over to his right, Tom strolling beside him.

"I come bearing gifts." He holds up a bottle of wine in each hand. "What's a party without a little alcohol?"

"Oh my God, I love you so much right now." I surge forward and snag one of the bottles from him, turning to Leah, a wide grin on my face. "Have I told you lately how much I adore your brother?" I stop in place when I notice her attention is focused on the far wall. The wall lined with windows looking out over the back yard.

"Hell's bells. He's smoking hot, Megs." She continues to stare out the window, stepping closer as she does.

"Um, husband here." Tyler calls out, reminding her of his presence.

"No one is hotter than you babe." Her head swings momentarily back to him as she flashes a quick smile his way, then turns back to the window. "But you can't deny that is one fine piece of male specimen out there."

"Still here." Tyler chuckles. "And do you maybe want to say hello to your brother?"

"Hey, Tom." Leah tosses out.

"Love you too, Sis." Tom laughs, walking over to the counter to set down the other bottle of wine, then walks over to me, taking the bottle I snagged a second ago. "I'll open it."

"Oh, thanks." I give him a smile then move to join Leah. I lower my voice to a whisper. "And yeah, he's still pretty fricking fine." We both break out in laughter, my mother muttering under her breath at our silliness.

"I'm going out there." Leah states.

My head snaps away from the window to her. "Absolutely not."

"I'm going." She starts moving toward the door at the end of the kitchen. "I'm going to find out what's going on here."

"Leah!" I chase after her. "He's here for Ben. That's what's going on here."

She stops and looks at me. "But what about you?"

I throw my hands up. "What about me?"

"How does he feel about you?" She persists.

"I have no idea." Which of course is a lie. If my instincts are right, he's still as attracted to me as I am to him. But I have no idea what his dating status is, or where his affections may lie now. "Besides, that doesn't matter. This is about Ben."

"Oh you silly friend." She shakes her head, giving me a pat on the cheek. "Of course it matters." And before I can stop her, she's out the door heading straight for Jasper. I stand, frozen, like my feet are stuck in quicksand, and watch as she strolls right up to him. I keep watching, Ben's face lighting up when he sees Leah, jumping off the swing to run into her arms. Her talking to Ben for a few minutes before he runs over to the slide. Her shaking Jasper's hand. Her crossing her arms as she begins what I can only assume is her interrogation.

"Here, take this." Tom's voice is beside me, dragging my attention away from the scene in front of me, a glass of wine in his hand. "I think you're gonna need it." I take the glass from him, taking a gulp as he walks away, my head turning right back to Jasper and Leah.

Well, no one seems to be yelling, and so far, she doesn't seem to have drawn blood, so maybe it's going to be okay. *Oh wait. Shit.* I watch as Jasper shakes his head, his face flushing red as he throws his hands up, then turns and stomps away. What in the world did Leah just do? She calls to Ben, who goes to her instantly, and then a minute later, she's coming back through the door.

"What in the world did you say to him?" I take another swig of my wine, then place it on the counter as I unzip Ben's jacket.

"Nothing." She rolls her eyes. "Well, not nothing obviously." She snags my glass in her fingers and takes a sip of it. "I just asked him what his intentions were, and reminded him that he already-" She lowers her voice to a whisper as she speaks over Ben's head. "fucked you over once with Miss McPoppy Pants."

"Oh, for crying out loud." I point a finger at her. "You had no business discussing that with him." I glance at my mom. "Can you keep an eye on him?" Then swing my head back to Leah, shooting her a dark look. "I need to go clean this up."

"Of course." My mom nods, wiping her hands on a dish towel. "I got these boys here to help me too." She looks at Tom and Tyler. "Go!" She shoos me away.

I give Leah one last angry glare, then hustle for the front door, hoping I catch Jasper before he leaves.

Chapter Twenty

"Oh, thank god. You're still here."

I stop pacing and twist my head in the direction of the slamming front door. I kick my toe into the gravel of the driveway, nodding. "Only because I didn't say goodbye to Ben."

I try to keep the anger from my voice, because what her friend just did to me isn't Megan's fault, but I know it still has an edge to it. "What the hell was that?" I point to the house, to her friend inside it. "If you want to know something about me and Poppy, all you have to do is ask. I'm not trying to keep anything from you, and I never did."

"I know." She's reached me now, and crosses her arms over her chest, hugging herself. "I'm sorry. She's just being protective."

"You don't have a jacket." I frown, then open the hatch on the back of the Porsche. I reach into one of the boxes I have stowed there and pull out a sweatshirt. "Come here."

She takes a step closer, watching as I gather the sweatshirt in a way that I can help her put it on. She releases the hold she has on herself, then raises her hands, slipping them into the center of the material as I slide it completely over her.

"Thank you." She tilts her head so she can read the front of the sweatshirt, then looks back at me. It's got my name and number on it. Her hair is tousled and she's smiling. She always did look good wearing my number, but right now she's never looked more beautiful to me.

"I'm not a complete dick." I shrug, jerking my chin toward the house. "Contrary to what your friend in there thinks." I move to sit on the bumper of the Porsche, patting next to me, inviting her to sit as well. "I do care about you."

"Like I said, she's protective of me, and she doesn't want to see me get hurt again." She scoots up onto the bumper next to me, then turns to look at me. "My heart was pretty shattered after our time in Los Angeles, and Leah was the one that had to watch me process all that."

I frown, watching as she picks at her fingernails. "I don't know how many more times I can apologize to you until you believe that I'm sorry for what happened."

"I believe you." One side of her mouth slides up into a small smile. "I do." She shrugs. "We're just going to have to figure out where we go from here."

"Well, does it really matter how I feel or what I want when it comes to you?" I stare at the house. "Looks like the job of boyfriend is taken."

"What are you talking abo-" I twist my head, just in time to see her eyes widen. "Oh! You mean Tom?" She covers her mouth as laughter escapes, my brows furrowing in confusion.

"What's so funny?"

"Tom is so not my boyfriend. He's Leah's big brother and I've known him for ten years. We're just friends." She folds her hands in her lap, looking over at me. "And that's what I think you and I should try and be." She shrugs. "At least, that's what I'd like."

I nod, bending my head down in an attempt to hide the smile that erupts on my face the second she said Tom's not her boyfriend. "Friends would be great." *For now.*

"So, you always keep boxes of sweatshirts just lying around in the back of your truck?" She looks over her shoulder at the boxes there.

I chuckle, standing up to turn and look in the trunk. "I have an online store. We sell a ton of merchandise that way, but I usually have some with me for events that I pop into and stuff like that."

"That's cool." She jumps off the bumper then pulls one of the boxes closer and pops open the lid. "You got anything else in here I might like?"

"You can take whatever you want." *Including me if that's in the cards.*

She stops rifling through the box and turns to look at me. "So, you're still playing football?"

My eyes pop wide. "You really don't go on the internet, do you?"

"Nope." She shakes her head. "Crazy but true."

"Not so much crazy, but rare these days." I scrub at the scruff on my chin. "But to answer your question, yes, I'm still playing football. I'd like to get one more ring before I retire. But either way, this year will most likely be my last."

"How come?" She pulls out a pom-pom hat with my logo on it and pulls it on her head.

"I'm going to be thirty-four this year. My body is tired." I bat at the pom-pom on the top of the hat, smiling as I do. "I don't want to get hurt so bad that I can't get out of bed in another ten years without being in pain."

"Well, I promise Ben and I will watch all your games this year."

"I'll get you both season tickets. You can come to a game anytime you want. I'd love to have you there."

"That sounds great." She looks toward the house, one side of her mouth drifting down. "Guess we should go back in there."

I let out a heavy sigh. "Yeah, guess so."

"Don't worry, I'll call off Leah." She promises, then taps the hat on her head. "Can I keep this?"

"Of course." I slide the other box closer, rummage through it, and pull out a child's sweatshirt. "For Ben."

We go back inside, and as promised, she has a chat with Leah. The rest of the afternoon goes by in a blur, but with much less hostility. I spend more time with Ben, feed him dinner, help give him a bath, and the best part, read him some stories before putting him to bed. When I step out of his room, I ease the door close, startled when I turn around to find Megan leaning against the wall of the hallway. *Wow.* She's changed into a short white, sleeveless dress that's lacey. Her hair is curly, and she's wearing deep red lipstick, something I've never seen on her before. It's sexy as hell and makes me want to slam my mouth against hers. "You look gorgeous."

She pushes off the wall, then takes a few steps, closing the distance between us. She stops when she reaches me, the nude colored-high heels she's wearing making it easier to look into her eyes. "It's actually a gift from my mom. I know it's a bit extravagant for a dinner with friends, but it will make her happy to see me wearing it."

"It's your birthday celebration, but you want to make other people happy?" I muse, unable to stop myself from brushing my fingers down the soft skin of her arm until they link with her fingers.

"It's an easy thing to do." She murmurs, her head tilting as she follows the path of my touch, swinging back up to meet my gaze when I join our hands. She stares at me, her tongue, so pink in contrast to the color of her mouth, darts out to pull her bottom lip between her teeth.

Lifting my other hand, I use my thumb to tug her lip free, her breath hot as it floats over my knuckle. "God I want to kiss you right now." My voice is husky as my hand drifts across her cheek, then wraps around the base of her neck, her eyes never leaving mine as her head arches into my palm.

Her pulse drums under my touch, and she finally blinks, her voice a whisper as she grants her permission. "I'm not stopping you."

I tighten the hold I have on her hand as I slide it around her back, hauling her body up against mine, inhaling her citrusy scent as I lower my mouth to hers.

"Meghan, where are you?" Her mother's loud shrill

sounds from the bottom of the stairs. "Everyone is waiting down here."

I freeze, our faces so close I can feel the heat of her flaring cheeks a second before she pushes away from me, muttering under her breath. "Great timing Mom." We free ourselves from each other, her eyes dashing to mine and then away as she starts for the stairs. "Sorry."

"Me too." Not really, but I don't want to make her feel any more uncomfortable, so I say what I think she wants to hear. I almost run into her when she stops short and turns to me.

"Sorry about my mother." She clarifies, speaking low. Her eyes cut to my mouth again. "Not that you almost kissed me." Then she spins around, skipping down the steps, addressing her mother before I can respond. "Coming, Mother."

"Oh, don't you look lovely!" Sandy exclaims as her daughter reaches her, her brow furrowing when Megan brushes quickly by her. Her eyes cut to me, a knowing look registering on her face as I scoot past her.

"Sorry about that. We were just finishing up with Ben." I sputter out the first excuse I can think of.

"Uh-huh." She drawls, following behind me. "If you say so." Relief surges through me when I hear her chuckle lightly.

Dinner ends up being really nice, and I'm glad I stayed. I'm seated directly across from Megan, which normally would have been fine. If she didn't look so damn sexy. If I didn't constantly want to touch her. If every time she laughed I didn't want to swallow her whole. Every single thing I had felt for her in Los Angeles still lived in me, and has only seemed to intensify now that I was with her again. When I arrived here today, all I wanted was to get to know my son and be a part of his life. In one day's time, I realize my life will only be complete if she's in it too.

Chapter Twenty-One

Every time I look across the table at Jasper, pings of electricity zap throughout my body, every nerve ending tingling. He just looks at me and makes me feel so desired, so much like a woman, reminding me of the time we spent in Los Angeles. Never has anyone ever made me feel the way that he did, and being in the same space with him is stirring it all to the surface. And with every glance, every brush of our fingers, every word we share, it's bringing that simmering heat between us to a boil.

"Should we go into the living room and have some more wine?" I suggest, now that dinner is over and my mother has thoroughly embarrassed me with a large cake. It was its own fire hazard she had so many candles lit, as she and all my friends sang me Happy Birthday.

"You kids go ahead." My mom speaks first. "I'm going to head to bed. It's been a long day for me."

We all wish her good night and then the rest of us

transfer to the other room, Tom and Tyler each carrying a bottle of wine with them. I wait until everyone finds a seat, and then settle myself in last. I make sure to not sit next to Jasper. And not because I don't want to. That's the problem. I want to more than anything. I'd like to crawl into his lap and curl up like a kitten. I'm quite sure I'd probably start purring too. So, in order to keep from making a complete fool of myself, I place myself on the opposite side of the couch from him.

Tom has another glass of wine, then excuses himself, citing an early morning departure for a client meeting he has in the morning. He's a sports agent, and there's an up and coming baseball player that needs representation. Tom's going to the game in the city tomorrow, but wants to prep beforehand at his office.

"Thank you again for coming." I move to rise off the couch, but he motions for me to stay. He bends, placing a kiss on my cheek.

"I wouldn't have missed it." He shares a look with me that only I can decipher, then whispers against my cheek so no one else can hear. "He's a lucky bastard." He's standing before I can reply, so I just give him a smile that I hope expresses what his friendship means to me. He shakes Jasper's hand, says something to him I can't hear, then moves quickly on to Tyler and his sister, giving them both a hug before leaving the room.

"How long will you be home for this time Tyler?" I ask, wondering how long I'll have my best friend around for before they leave on another adventure.

"Three weeks I think?" He looks over at Leah for confirmation, who nods her head. "I have to be out in Los Angeles to record some new tracks. We wrote some great stuff while we were on the road and we want to lay it down while it's still fresh for us."

"Three weeks?" I whine, shifting my attention to Leah. "That's not nearly enough time! I'm just going to get used to you being here and you'll leave me again." I push my bottom lip out in an exaggerated pout. "And poor Ben; he never gets to see his Godmother anymore." Yes, I'm trying to make her feel guilty, but only because I've missed having her by my side for, well, for everything.

"We'll only be gone two weeks I think." She defends, then swivels her body toward me. "What if I take Ben next weekend? I'd love to spend some time with him, and then you can spoil yourself rotten with a couple days off? It will be my bonus birthday present to you." She looks at Tyler for confirmation. "That's okay with you, right honey?"

"Sure." He shrugs. "I love having the little guy around."

I shift my eyes to Jasper to gauge his reaction. We haven't discussed what our schedule will be, and how often he'd like to see his son. I feel like I've already taken so much away from him by not telling him I was pregnant, so I want to make sure I give him a chance to weigh in on decisions about him now. "Jasper? Would you mind that? I'm not sure if you wanted to see him again next weekend?"

He's quiet for several long seconds, but then nods once. "Sure." He takes a drink from his wine glass, keeping eye contact with me while he does, then speaks again. "You and I can talk tomorrow to figure out when I can see Ben."

"Yay!" Leah claps in delight. "And I promise bestie, I'll

spend so much time with you over the next few weeks, you'll be so sick of me."

"Never." I grin at her. "Impossible."

"On that note, I think I'll hit the hay." Tyler places his empty wine glass on the table closest to him, then stands, raising his arms in a long stretch as he yawns. "I'm frigging beat."

Leah bounces up beside him, sliding an arm around his waist, delivering a flirty wink. "Come on. I'll tuck you in."

"Good night you love birds." I sing-song to them as they drift toward the stairs.

"Nighty-night." Leah leans over the railing as they begin climbing upwards, giggling. "Don't do anything I wouldn't do."

I'm about to respond, but turn my attention away when I feel Jasper slide down the length of the couch until he's almost touching me. I grip my wine glass with both hands as I lift it to my mouth, hoping he can't see them trembling.

"Alone at last." He raises his own glass, tilting it back as he finishes what's left in it, then leans forward to place it on the table in front of us. Without saying a word, he slips my glass from my fingers, then places it next to his.

"What are you doing?" I cringe when I hear the slight shake to my voice. I'm not afraid of him, Not even a little bit. And it's not nerves. It takes me a second to realize that it's excitement. To be this close to him again, and to know without a doubt that I want him, and that he still wants me.

"Nothing, if you don't want me to." He scoots a fraction closer, his fingers skimming over my knee before resting on my thigh, his thumb sweeping back and forth. "But I've been waiting for over three hours for the chance to try and kiss you again." He leans toward me, my eyes locking onto his tongue as it swipes across his lips leaving them glistening and wet. "Tell me to stop and I will."

I shake my head, then propel myself forward until my mouth crashes into his, my arms coiling around his neck. His arms band around my waist, lifting me until I'm straddling him, our bodies pressing together as our kissing becomes almost frantic. His hands move to cradle my face as his lips leave mine and begin to rain small pecks on my cheeks, my nose, my eye lids. Between each kiss, he speaks a single word. "Missed. You. Missed. This. Want. You. Want. This." His lips find mine again, passion consuming us both as our tongues slide together, a groan rumbling up from his chest when I grind my core against his hard length.

He tears his face back, his chest heaving against mine as he pants, his caramel irises locking onto my confused expression. "What is it?" I pant out, my hand sliding up to cup his cheek. I'm still not used to seeing him without his beard, but kissing him is even stranger. It's more bristled, but it's still soft against my palm.

"We should slow down." He chuckles, giving a slight shake of his head. "I can't believe I'm going to say this, but it feels a little weird doing this with your mom right above us."

I'm about to argue, but freeze, my brows raising in alarm as I cock my head to make sure I wasn't imagining things. "Mommy?" Nope. Wasn't my imagination. I push off Jasper to stand in one swift motion, looking down at him. "Ben is awake."

He's standing beside me before I can blink. "Are you sure?" As if answering his question on cue, Ben calls out for me again, louder this time. "Mommy?"

"I'm here honey." I call out, giving Jasper's arm a light squeeze as I hurry for the stairs. He's still not good on them and I don't want him to try and go down them in the dark. "Stay there, Mommy's coming." I fly up the stairs, Jasper on my heels, and find Ben standing outside the door to my bedroom, his fists rubbing his eyes as he tries to focus. "What's a matter Bugaboo?"

"I woked up." He mumbles, leaning into my body as I pick him up.

"Okay, let's see if we can get you back to sleep." I stroke a hand gently over his back. "You want to sleep in my room with me?"

"Okay." He says, his little mouth forming an O as he lets out a silent yawn.

I look up to find Jasper staring at us, my heart skipping a beat at the expression on his face. It's pure, unfiltered love shining from him. It takes my breath away when I realize the feelings we had for each other never really went away. We both just stored them away in a box, trying our best to forget about them. I open my mouth to speak, but can't seem to find the right words, then snap it shut, only to open it to try again.

"It's okay." He smooths his hand over mine on Ben's back, and then drops a kiss against the back of his downy locks. "I'll see you in the morning. Get some sleep."

"Okay." I finally manage. "Good night."

In the morning, Jasper and Ben play together after breakfast, Ben passing out immediately when I put him down for his nap at eleven. Tyler and Leah left after breakfast, so Jasper and I take the quiet time to sit down and figure out what's next for us. Well, at least when it comes to Ben.

"I work during the week, and Ben goes to a really nice daycare." I take a sip of the coffee I made for each of us, then continue. "If I have to travel to a client site, my mom will either come with us, or he'll stay here with her, depending on how long I need to be gone for. I don't like to leave him for more than three days."

He leans back in the chair, his chest heaving as he takes a deep breath. "I was actually in Boston because of the marathon tomorrow. I'm supposed to fly back home on Wednesday." He frowns, his fingers tracing the rim of the coffee cup in front of him.

"Oh." I digest what he just revealed. "So, by home, you mean California?"

"During the off season, yeah. I usually don't come back to Boston until late June when training starts again." He nods, looking directly at me. "Obviously this changes things for me. And to be honest, I haven't thought about what comes next because I wasn't sure how coming to see him yesterday was going to go."

"And now?" I shift forward, folding my hands on the table.

"And now I just need a few days to figure it all out." He leans forward, putting his hands over mine when I start to slide back. "I want to be a part of his life. There's absolutely no doubt about that. I want to be his father."

"But?" I arch a brow, because I know it's coming and just want him to spit it out.

"But I just found out I had a child four days ago. It's a lot." He looks over my shoulder for a second, then continues. "All I'm asking for is a little time to process that so I can figure out a new game plan for the next few months."

"Okay." What he's asking for is more than reasonable. He's been pretty gracious up to this point, and the very least I can do is meet him halfway.

"That's it?" His brow furrows.

"What else do you want me to say?" I slide my hands out from under his so I can lean back in my chair.

"It just seems too easy." He shrugs, a crooked grin on his face. "I'm waiting for the other shoe to drop."

"Jasper, what you're asking for isn't much." I lift my hands, palms up, in front of me. "A little time is fine." I settle my hands back in my lap, looking down at them as I ask the next thing of him. "Just promise me you'll come back?"

His chair scrapes back as he rises, then kneels beside me, pulling my hands into his. "Megan, I promise." He squeezes my fingers gently. "Hey, look at me." I lift my gaze, trailing slowly up until I lock onto his, remaining silent, even though my heart is pounding loud enough to announce my fear. "I'll be back." He releases his hold, moving one hand to cup my cheek. "For both of you."

Chapter Twenty-Two

After driving around the block five times, I'm finally able to snag a parking spot only a half-block away from the building number she gave me. It was probably a bad idea to drive into the city, but when I left Boston, it seemed like a good idea. At least easier in terms of bringing with me what I needed. I glance at the clock on the dash of the Porsche. Just a little after five. Hopefully she's home. It is a Saturday night, and it is her actual birthday, so there's no saying for sure if she'll even be here. I know I'm taking a chance. The one thing I know for sure is that Ben is with Leah and Tyler tonight, so if she is home, we might actually get some time alone.

I hop out of the SUV, then open the back door to gather the items I brought with me. I kick the door shut with my foot, then head down the sidewalk until I reach her building. There's a doorman outside, which surprises me a little. I wasn't expecting her to live in such a nice area of the city, but I guess there's still a lot about her I don't know, including her financial situation. The doorman holds the door wide when he sees me, addressing me once I'm in the lobby. "Good evening, Sir."

"Hi." I give him a nod. Before I can ask if Megan is home, he starts talking again.

"Aren't you Jasper Chase?" He scratches his chin as he stares at me, cocking his head in examination. "From the Patriots?"

"Yeah." I shuffle in place, my load getting a little heavy. "Hey man, I'd be happy to sign something if you want, and even take a picture, but could you tell me first if Megan Lewis is home?"

"Well, normally I wouldn't reveal that kind of information, but-" His eyes widen like the reason is obvious. "you're Jasper Chase!" His voice rises in excitement as he says my name. God damn. Any other time this wouldn't bother me at all, but I'm nervous as hell showing up here without telling her and just want to get this part over with. "But, yes, Ms. Lewis is home. Should I announce you?"

"No, she's expecting me." One little white lie wasn't going to hurt. "Can you just get the elevator for me?" I look down at my full hands, hoping the reason for the assist is obvious.

"Of course." He strides over to the elevator, pressing the up arrow, the door opening immediately. "Here you go." He keeps his hand against one side of the door as I enter, then reaches around the corner to hit the button marked eleven. I smile, taking some small satisfaction in her floor number being the same as my jersey number. I'll take that as a good omen. "Have a good night, Mr. Chase."

"Thanks." I reply, then call out as the doors start to slide shut. "I'll give you that autograph on the way out!"

A minute later, the doors slide open and I step out into the hallway. I look in both directions, noting there's only six doors total, and decide to try going right first. I get lucky, the second door I come to, marked with a B, the apartment letter she wrote down in the information she gave me last weekend. I take a deep breath, steeling myself for whatever happens next, and then use my knuckles to knock on the door. I hear some rustling on the other side of the door, then the view slide moving, snapping closed quickly a second later. *Guess she knows I'm here.* I hear two locks turning, then the door swings open, Megan standing in the doorway a wide-eyed expression on her face.

"What in the world are you doing here?" Her hands are planted on her hips, but there's a bright smile lighting up her expression, so I don't think she's mad.

"I told you I'd be back." I hold up the bottle of Veuve I have in one hand, then extend the bouquet of roses I have in the other. "I thought maybe we could start over from the beginning?" I shrug, one side of my mouth lifting in a hopeful smile. "Plus, it's your thirtieth birthday."

She wraps her fingers around the roses, sliding them out of my grasp, her lids closing as she brings them to her face and inhales. "These are beautiful." She opens her eyes and steps back, motioning for me to come in. "It's a mess. I wasn't expecting anyone, and thought I had tomorrow morning to clean before Ben gets back."

"I don't care how messy your home is." I look around, noting that it seems neat as a pin, just like her hotel room back in the day. "I didn't want to wait any longer to see you. I hope its okay that I'm here."

"It's more than okay." She shuts the door after I walk through, then spins around. "You didn't go back to California?"

"No." I shake my head. "I couldn't leave. Everything I want and need is here."

"Oh." Her cheeks flush the adorable pink I've come to love, her feet shuffling in place.

"I made reservations at The Palm." I babble on, my nerves getting the best of me. "It's different than the one in L.A., but yeah, if you want, we can go." I shrug, finally shutting my trap when I notice she's standing in front of me again.

"I'd rather stay in." Her voice is low as one corner of her mouth ticks up in a suggestive smile.

"We can stay in." *We can do whatever the hell you want. Just don't ask me to leave.*

"We can order take-out." She suggests, moving across the room now to place the flowers on a counter framing the kitchen. The apartment is a large, rectangle open space, the kitchen on one side, and a huge living room on the other. There are three doors on the far end of the wall, which I assume are bedrooms and a bathroom. It's decorated in a lot of creams and blues, large area rugs are placed strategically across the shiny wood floors.

"This is a really nice home." I tread slowly into the large

space until I'm next to Megan at the counter, and hand her the bottle. "Happy Birthday."

"Thank you." She smiles. "But you really didn't have to bring me anything." She shrugs. "We all celebrated last weekend."

"But I didn't know it was your birthday, and what's a birthday without a gift?" My mouth crooks up in a smile.

"These are beautiful." She runs a hand down the roses, turning her head to look at them, then swinging it back to me a second later, her mouth dropping open. "Oh!"

"Those weren't your presents." I'm holding out a small, wrapped box, which she takes, her eyes crinkling around the edges as she smiles even wider.

"You got me a present?" She starts tearing at the paper, her head snapping up to mine when she recognizes the light blue box. "Tiffany's?" She laughs nervously. "It's not an engagement ring, right?" Her fingers shaking just a tiny bit as she fumbles with the ribbon.

"Don't think we're quite there." *Yet.* I leave that part off, because I don't want to totally freak her out, but it's definitely something I can picture with her; forever. It was a feeling I had when we were together four years ago and being with her again is just reinforcing it. She finally gets the ribbon off and lifts the lid to the box, her eyes sweeping up to mine.

"Jasper, it's too much." She traces a finger over the delicate chain of the necklace.

"It's not enough." I step closer to her, pointing to two keys on the chain, one tiny yellow key, and then a larger key with white and yellow diamonds embedded throughout.

"Those represent you and Ben to me. You both hold the keys to my heart now. You both decide where we go from here." I place a finger under her chin and lift it until our gazes lock. "But I'm all in. For whatever you want."

She blinks rapidly, her chin starting to tremble under my touch before she surges forward to wrap her arms around my neck in a hug. "You keep saying and doing all the right things. But I'm so scared." She tightens her hold as she keeps whispering in my ear. "So scared we're going to mess this up again."

"We won't." I slide my arms around her, enveloping her tiny frame in my large one to hold her as close as I can. "We'll take it slow. One day at a time. And we'll make sure we talk to each other this time. No matter what. No assumptions. No letting anyone else get between us." I pull back from her so I can look into her eyes. "I'm not losing you again. And I'm pretty sure I've been in love with you since the moment I ran into you at that hotel in Los Angeles."

"Jasper." Her voice is a surprised whisper as tears start to trickle down her cheeks. "This seems too easy."

"What?" I chuckle, my brows shooting up. "None of this has been easy." I grin down at her. "It's taken us almost four years to get here."

"Good point." She giggles through the tears, her expression growing more serious when she stops. "I want it all with you Jasper. And I know we have a lot to figure out." She nods, rolling her eyes to indicate just how much. "But I think I'm in love with you." She nods again, tears still falling from her eyes. "And I want to try if you do."

My heart swells at her revelation, feeling whole again for the first time in years. I always thought football would be the only thing I needed to feel complete. I had no idea until this very moment how incomplete I was until I heard her say she loves me. *She loves me!* I sweep her back against me, lowering my mouth against hers, sealing our love with a kiss, hoping that this is just the beginning of the love and happiness to come for us.

Epilogue

Nine Months Later...

"Oh my god! Oh my god! Yay!" I jump up and down, clapping my hands wildly as I look over at Leah and Tyler on one side of me, and Jasper's family on the other, Ben standing in front of me. "We won! We're Super Bowl Champions!"

"Stop jumping around like that!" Leah admonishes, a wide grin on her face as she looks down at my swollen stomach. "That poor baby's getting all jumbled around in there!"

I look down, my engagement ring shimmering as I lay a hand over my expanding belly. We found out at Christmas we're having a little girl. She's due at the end of March. Perfect timing for all of us. Jasper has already decided to retire after this season, his dream of winning one more Super Bowl now achieved. He's going to take a year off, then figure out what's next for him. Most likely he'll go into sports casting for one of the football networks. They've already been scouting him, rumors flying around about his retirement announcement.

We're planning a June wedding. It will be enough time after the baby comes that hopefully my figure will be somewhat back to normal. Jasper wanted to get married the minute he found out I was pregnant again, but the last thing I wanted was a big belly under my wedding dress. We both decided an outside ceremony is what we wanted, and we're trying to pull it off on the beach we visited the week we met. We're not sure if there will be a dozen helicopters overhead, but so far, we think we're keeping the location under wraps. It's a whole new way of life trying to get used to being in a relationship with someone that's recognized, but we're adjusting. The flurry after the world discovered Jasper had a 'love child' was a bit overwhelming, but we made it through.

Jasper's been jumping between Boston and New York during the entire season, but now that it's over, we're going to relocate to his home in California. We spent a lot of time there last summer, and Ben and I both fell in love with it there. I left my job at the end of the year, a little hesitant after working so hard to establish my career, but knowing in my heart it was the right thing for me. My family is my number one priority now. I've never been happier and know I can always go back if I decide that's what I want. My mother obviously isn't very happy that we're relocating, but the California house is huge, and we've already set aside a room for her.

"Mommy, let's go see Daddy!" Ben jumps up and down,

one hand tugging at the sleeve of my jersey, as he pulls me toward the door.

"Okay, okay." I take his hand, leading him out of the box we're in, following his family down to the field. It's complete chaos, everyone pushing and shoving as they try and reach the players on the team. I pull Ben a little closer, but then smile in relief when Jasper's dad takes him and swings him up on his shoulders.

"Do you see your dad, Bud?" He calls up to him through the roar of the crowd.

"I see him Poppa!" He wiggles around, excitement shining on his face, as he points in the direction we should go. "Right there!"

We all surge forward, finally breaking through the crowd into an inner circle. Jasper's talking to a reporter, but stops as soon as he sees us, a huge smile lighting up his face. He says something to the man, then starts sprinting in our direction. I can't help myself, and break into a run, launching myself into his arms, my future, and the beginning of our happily ever after.

The End

Afterword

Thank you so much for reading Catching Chase.
If you enjoyed this book, you'll probably love Losing Hope.

It features Hope Yorke, a beautiful, successful, executive who's just had her heart broken. After walking in on her boyfriend getting intimate with someone else, she escapes to her family lake house in Vermont.

A chance encounter with handsome, ex-marine, Gage Flynn, turns her weekend into something completely unexpected. She thinks she may have met the man of her dreams until he discovers who her family is and walks away. How does she pick up the pieces and keep herself from losing hope?

Keep flipping the pages, I've got an excerpt of the entire first chapter for you.
Already hooked?

Afterword

You can download it for any platform using this link:
Universal Link: books2read.com/u/brYoyY

If you like things just a little bit steamier, you can also check out my book, The Winning Bid. It's book one of The Auction Duet, and it's absolutely free on any platform. Universal Link: books2read.com/u/mey2KZ

Sneak Peek

LOSING HOPE

Chapter One

Hope Yorke was not having a good morning. It started when her alarm clock didn't go off, causing her to bolt upright in bed when the doorman called to let her know her car had arrived. After the fastest shower ever, and the heaviest morning traffic in ages, things only got worse. Just as she walked out of Starbucks, some asshole slammed into her, causing her scalding hot latte to spill down the front of her black Donna Karan wrap dress and drip all the way down onto her brand new pink satin Louboutin heels.

She had waited three months for those shoes to come in on back order from Paris. Thankfully, she always kept several spare outfits in her office, so after another quick shower and change of clothes—a royal blue Calvin Klein belted Ponte knit dress with a black pair of Jimmy Choo suede pumps—she walked into the company board meeting quite late, a meeting in which her father sat at the head of the table. Taking her seat to his right, she didn't miss the look of disappointment that flashed across his stern features as he nodded to her.

"Nice of you to join us, Hope."

"My apologies to you all." She glanced around the table, making eye contact with each board member at the table. She may be the boss's daughter, but she expected no special treatment and had earned her right to sit at this table. Hope had graduated with honors from Columbia University with a major in Business Management and a minor in English and Comparative Literature, and for the last six years, she had worked her way up through the ranks of her father's publishing company. At only twenty-eight years old, she was proud to be the youngest ever Senior Vice President of US Publishing to sit at this table.

"I had a small accident on my way in this morning."

Her father's hand immediately reached out and covered hers as he asked quietly, "Are you all right, Hope?"

She nodded and smiled at him in return. "Yes, Father, I'm fine." She patted his hand and then, addressing the board, continued, "If someone will just catch me up, let's continue with the meeting."

The meeting lasted well past lunch and into the afternoon, so by the time Hope was back in her office, she had endless emails and messages to return. She was off to her lake house in Vermont that evening, and the sooner she could get through things, the sooner she could get on the road.

Several hours later, Emily, Hope's assistant, stood in the

entrance to her office. "Excuse me, Miss Yorke, it's after five. Billy is on the phone and wants to know if you'll still require the helicopter this evening, or if you've changed your mind about heading North?"

"Shit!" Jumping up, she gathered her computer and paperwork and stuffed them into her bag. "I had no idea it had gotten so late! Yes, please ask Billy to wait, and can you also have Ed bring the car around to the front? It's faster if we leave from there instead of the garage entrance."

"Of course, Miss Yorke." Emily was out the door and back at her desk making the necessary calls before Hope could say another word.

Quickly pulling on her trench coat, she grabbed her bags and headed to take the elevator down to the lobby as fast as her heels would allow. She walked outside into the chilly fall air to find Ed waiting for her at the curb beside the car. He tipped his head in greeting. "Miss Yorke. Seaport Helipad?"

Giving him a nod, she handed him her computer bag. "Yes, please, Ed, the quicker the better. I completely lost track of time."

She climbed into the back as he closed the door behind her. The car carried a light scent of the Old Spice aftershave he always wore, which Hope thought was better than any air freshener that could have been used. She heard him load her bag into the trunk, and then he was in the driver's seat and pulling smoothly into traffic. "I'll get you there as quick as I can, Miss. Traffic's a little heavy right now, it being Friday night and all."

"Thank you again, Ed. Billy's waiting at the helipad for me, so I appreciate it."

"Just you going up North this weekend, Miss?" Weathered blue eyes looked at her in question from the rear-view mirror.

"Yep, just me. Need a bit of a break from everything."

Ed knew it was a little more than that. He knew that almost two weeks ago she'd come back early from a business trip and, instead of going home, had decided to surprise her boyfriend of two years at his place. The surprise was on her, though, when she walked in and found him screwing some redhead on the kitchen counter. Ed knew this because he was behind her with her bags. He was also the one to cold-cock that prick Dylan in the chin when he ran after her as she turned and fled. He then listened to her cry in the backseat of the car as he drove her back to her apartment. Yeah, Ed knew she needed a little break all right.

They reached the heliport, and Ed helped her out of the car and grabbed her computer bag from the trunk. After entering the terminal and confirming their identities, Ed walked with Hope to the helipad where Billy was waiting next to the helicopter. He smiled wide at Hope and nodded to Ed in greeting as he walked out to meet them.

"We're all set to go, Miss Yorke. I'm sorry I can't take you all the way up this time. Tower says the rain and wind are a bit too strong to take the chopper."

"It's no problem at all, Billy. At least we can still take the plane." Hope was getting seated in the chopper now, with Billy making sure her straps were buckled securely. He circled around the chopper, hopped in on his side, and strapped himself in.

"It should be a quick fifteen minutes over to the airport. The plane is ready and waiting for you at the terminal."

Hope nodded in acknowledgment as the chopper took flight over the river and then banked to the left toward LaGuardia. These were the perks of being a Yorke. Hope had private helicopters and planes to take her wherever she needed to go, when she wanted to go, and this weekend, all she wanted was some time to herself. She was looking forward to curling up with a book in front of the fire, drinking wine, sleeping late, going for long walks around the lake, and just forgetting about the last couple of weeks.

What a prick Dylan turned out to be. She knew she wasn't in love him and probably wouldn't ever have married him. But still, what happened to having a little respect and just breaking things off with someone, instead of cheating on them? They were supposed to be damn grownups, after all. Humiliation still burned in her gut. Of course, within hours, there were endless deliveries of flowers and calls from Dylan asking for forgiveness. After one phone call back, calmly telling him to go fuck himself, or better yet, the redhead, she threw herself into her work, putting in sixteen-hour days to try to numb the pain of her new reality. That was almost two weeks ago, and the long days had caught up with her.

As promised, fifteen minutes later, they landed at LaGuardia. A shuttle was waiting to drive her over to the private terminal where the company jet was housed. Upon arrival, she boarded the plane and made herself comfortable in one of the white leather seats.

"Good evening, Miss Yorke. It's nice to see you." Sylvia,

one of the regular flight attendants on board, seemed to appear from nowhere, ready to make sure Hope was comfortable and didn't need anything.

"Hello, Sylvia. Nice to see you, as well. Do you think you could get me some coffee?"

"Of course. Are you hungry? I can make you anything on the menu."

"Just the coffee for now. Thank you."

Sylvia smiled and made her way to the small galley.

The Captain boarded the plane and greeted Hope with a warm smile. "All pre-checks are done, Miss. We can leave as soon as the tower gives us clearance."

"Wonderful, Glenn. Thank you." Sylvia appeared and handed Hope a mug of freshly brewed coffee, of course, prepared exactly to her liking, and then disappeared back in the galley.

"There's a pretty good storm going on from Montpelier and up through Canada, so things may get a little bumpy at the tail end of our flight."

Her brow furrowed. "Any reason to be concerned or delay my flight?"

"We'll get you there no problem. Your father would have my neck in a noose if I did anything to harm his most precious asset." He gave her a friendly wink and headed to the cockpit.

Several minutes later, they were in the air and leaving the island of Manhattan behind. She felt lighter and lighter as the distance between her and the city grew. Going up to the lake house was her sanctuary, and she couldn't wait to get there. Her grandfather had built the house on Lake

Champlain over seventy years ago. It wasn't an extravagant house in any way. In fact, it was the complete opposite of what her home and life were like in the city. The lake house was rustic, all wood and stone and everything a house on a country lake should be.

The first floor was one big open space that contained the kitchen, dining, and living room. The entire back side of the living room wall was made up of windows that overlooked a huge deck and, of course, the beautiful lake. There was a stone fireplace that made up one side wall in the living room and was surrounded by big, over-stuffed sofas. The sofas were strewn with throw pillows and lap blankets made of the softest fabrics. She loved to sit on those couches for hours just staring out at the lake, watching the world swim by.

Upstairs were four bedrooms, one on each corner of the house, with a bathroom on each side, between each room. The beds were still covered with quilts that Hope's grandmother had made by hand. Soft, thick rugs were on the wooden floors of each room, helping to keep toes warm on cold winter mornings. The master bedroom faced the lake and had another stone fireplace along the wall.

The only rooms in the house to be updated had been the bathrooms. Until she was around three, only cold water ran through the house, and the plumbing was limited. Her father had made it a priority to update the plumbing and bathroom fixtures, more for his comfort than anyone else's. Her mother had grown up at the lake house, so it had never bothered her. Her father did stay true to the style of the house, outfitting the bathrooms with beautiful claw foot bath tubs and antique vanities. The first time her mother took a hot bubble bath in one of the huge tubs, she had declared that perhaps this time her husband had been right.

Forty-five minutes later, a bit of turbulence jarred the plane, signaling their arrival at the edge of the storm. She sat up straighter, pulled her seatbelt tight, and prepared herself for a bumpy ride. When she lifted the shade on the window, splatters of wind-driven rain hit the glass, blackened by the night sky.

"We'll be landing in about twenty minutes, but it will be a rough few minutes. Can I get you anything before I buckle in?" Sylvia had magically appeared again.

"No, I'm fine. Thank you." She watched Sylvia sway back and forth from the turbulence as she made her way back to the front of the plane to secure herself for the rest of the flight.

She wasn't afraid of flying but wasn't particularly fond of being on a plane bouncing through the air at thirty thousand feet. She clutched onto the arm rests and counted the minutes until she heard the plane's landing gear descend. A few more drops and vicious sways, and the plane finally bounced onto the runway, wing flaps up and brakes squealing. Looking out the window again, Hope saw that the rain was pouring down and blowing sideways from the power of the wind. The plane slowly made its way to a private hanger, where it parked, a dry shelter from the storm.

Her Range Rover was parked in the hanger, and she thanked her lucky stars that she had driven it up here the last time she had visited. Her Mercedes S-Coupe wouldn't have handled the weather very well, but she had no doubt the Rover could. She unbuckled and gratefully accepted her trench coat from Sylvia.

"Are you sure you want to drive to the house in this weather, Miss Yorke? Maybe it would be better for you to stay in town tonight until the storm passes?" Sylvia questioned with nothing but concern.

"I'll be just fine." Smiling warmly, she patted her on the shoulder. "I have the Range Rover, and I know the roads like the back of my hand."

"Well, all right then. Will we be seeing you again for the ride back, or will you be driving down?"

"I haven't decided yet, but I'll make sure to let the team know by Sunday. I won't be leaving until Monday at the earliest."

Sylvia handed over her computer bag and purse then walked with her to the door. It had been opened and the stairs lowered for her exit.

"All right, Miss, please drive carefully, and as always, nothing but the best wishes for you."

"Thank you." Hope gave her a warm smile and started down the stairs. Glenn was waiting at the bottom to greet her.

"Sorry about the rough landing. Damn winds fought us every step of the way." He shook his head in frustration.

"Glenn, it was fine. We're all here in one piece." She walked toward the Rover.

"Well, the keys are in the Range Rover, and it's all gassed up for you. Maggie already stocked the house for you, so you should be fine once you get there."

"Wonderful. I'm not sure about my return plans yet, but

Sneak Peek

I'll let you and your team know as soon as I decide." Opening the rear door, she placed her computer bag and purse in the seat, taking her cell phone out to keep in the front with her.

"Very good. You just enjoy your time here, and we'll be ready if you need us."

"Thanks so much, Glenn." She gave him a quick peck on the cheek and climbed in behind the steering wheel.

"You be careful on those roads, Hope." He shut the door, hit the roof once with his palm, and walked away.

With a push of a button, the Rover roared to life, and she backed out of the hanger and headed toward the airport exit. The wipers were on at full blast as the rain pelted down and the wind whipped leaves and debris up from the road. Under normal circumstances, it generally took about thirty minutes to get to the lake house, but given the weather, she knew it might take longer. She hoped that the power hadn't been knocked out. It was a common occurrence around the lake when the weather turned bad.

She saw the sign for the highway entrance and merged to the right to enter. The highway was dark and wet, without another vehicle in sight. It was only a little after nine o'clock, but people must have been smarter than her, already at their homes, dry, and warm. The wipers continued to swish quickly back and forth, working hard to keep her view clear. She only had to be on the highway for one exit, but this far North, exits were about ten miles apart from each other. Reaching down, she turned the radio on but got nothing but static, so she hit the CD button and scrolled through until the fourth CD came up. "Round

Here" by the Counting Crows started playing over the speakers, and she sang along. This disc was one of her favorites and hadn't been taken out of the Rover since she purchased it.

Soon enough, she reached the exit and pulled off to merge onto Route 2. She was halfway to the house now, but this is where the roads got a little trickier. It was a simple two-lane road, curvy, and there wasn't a street light for miles. She knew the road well, though, and continued to sing her heart out as she drove through the storm, feeling safe in the sturdy SUV. Another fifteen minutes and she'd be there.

Want more?
Grab your copy right here:
Universal Link: books2read.com/u/brYoyY

About the Author

Michelle Windsor is a writer who lives north of Boston, Massachusetts, with her husband and two teenage boys.

She writes steamy contemporary romance, has achieved Amazon and Barnes & Noble International Best Seller status, and was awarded the Best Contemporary Romance Writer by Passionate Plume Ink in 2019.

When Michelle isn't working on another book, you can find her spending time with her family, her German Shepherd, Roman, or enjoying cocktails with her sisters and close-knit girlfriends.

You can find all Michelle's book on her website at https://www.authormichellewindsor.com

www.ingramcontent.com/pod-product-compliance
Lightning Source LLC
LaVergne TN
LVHW012038070526
838202LV00056B/5533